THE RIVER

and Other Stories

SEÁN MACKEL

First published in November 2010

Guildhall Press
Ráth Mór Business Park
Bligh's Lane
Derry
BT48 0LZ
Ireland

T: 00 44 28 7136 4413
F: 00 44 28 7137 2949
E: info@ghpress.com
W: www.ghpress.com

The author asserts his moral rights in this work in accordance with the Copyright, Designs and Patents Act 1998.

Typeset by Guildhall Press
Cover design and photography by Seán Mackel
Copyright © Seán Mackel/Guildhall Press
ISBN: 978 1 906271 33 6

A CIP record for this book is available from the British Library.

Guildhall Press gratefully acknowledges the financial support of the Arts Council of Northern Ireland as a principal funder under its Annual Support for Organisations Programme.

About the Author

Seán Mackel was born in Belfast in 1957. He now lives in the North West of Ireland. His poetry has appeared in *Cúirt Journal, Cyphers, HU, Poetry Ireland, Waterford Review* and *Four W*, Australia. A chapbook collection of his poetry, *Strangled Laughter*, was published by Lapwing Publications, Belfast, in 1998. *The River* is his first collection of short stories.

He held the post of Senior Lecturer in Graphic Design at CSU, Australia, and University of Ulster, Magee. In 2003, he established the first Master of Design in the UU. He was a key contributor to the formation of the UU School of Creative Arts in Derry. After over twenty years in education, he took early retirement in 2007.

As a visual artist, his work explores relationships between picture and text. He has exhibited in Australia and more recently in Ireland. His animated poem *1960 Belfast* was screened at the Belfast Film Festival, the Galway International Film Festival, the Irish Film Institute, 1997, and Triskel Arts Centre, Cork, 1998.

He is a director on the Board of Arts & Disability Forum.

Look … see the way the water is still moving underneath? It'll keep on moving. Only inches below … the owning is gone, even ours.

Colum McCann – *Zoli*

But how do we fashion the future? Who can say how except in the minds of those who will call it Now?

Miller Williams – *Of History and Hope*

Seán Mackel

THE RIVER
and Other Stories

GUILDHALL PRESS

In memory of my grandparents,
Mary-Ann and Joseph McKay,
Josephine and Seoirse Mackel

Acknowledgements

'Yellow Ochre' was short-listed for the Fish Short Story Prize (2003), Brian Moore Short Story Award (2003/4) and the Raymond Carver Short Story Contest (2004); it first appeared in *Carvezine.com* in November 2004. An early version of 'Ink Finding Paper' was published previously in *North West Anthology, Vol 5*. An early version of 'The Gap in the Door' (Rough Ground) was short-listed for the Michael McLaverty Short Story Award (2008).

First drafts of 'The Day Room', 'Ink Finding Paper', 'The River', 'Re-imagining Fish', 'The Jewel' (Dreaming of the Sea) and 'No Strings Attached' formed the basis of my Masters in Creative Writing thesis at the Seamus Heaney Centre (2008). Thanks to the academic team and in particular Ian Sansom for his generous advice and support during my time at QUB.

The following were useful references: the BBC website 'People's War' for 'The Day Room' and Simon O'Dwyer's *Prehistoric Music of Ireland* for 'Circular Breathing'.

Thanks and gratitude to Marilyn McLaughlin, editor on this, my first collection. Her insightful, honest and thorough criticism was invaluable.

I would also like to offer my thanks to Susanne Stich who, as always, has been a trusted sounding board for my writing. Thanks also to Nuala Ní Chonchúir for her encouragement, and to Sean O'Reilly for his advice and support and for contributing the foreword.

Thanks to my fellow writers during *The Stinging Fly* novel-writing workshops held at the Irish Writers' Centre during 2009–10. Thanks also to Finbar Dennis for his critical comments over many years.

Thanks also to my family; my parents, Phylis and Seán, my partner Susanne, and my children Méabh, Conor and Fiachra, for their understanding and support.

Finally, I would like to thank Paul, Declan, Kevin, Joe, Jenni and all at Guildhall Press.

SEÁN MACKEL
Derry, 2010

CONTENTS

FOREWORD

On the shoreline between Moville and Greencastle, a young man rinses a didgeridoo with water from the Foyle and begins to play. The technique used to produce the distinctive unbroken sound from the instrument is known as circular breathing. The young man is a white Aboriginal and he has travelled across the world on a promise made to an old woman native to the Inishowen area who looked after him as a child. In his bag he carries a book of poems, one of which says, *I know this little now, this accidental present is not all of me.*

This thought could serve as the message at the heart of this collection of subtly interconnected stories. There is much more to each and every one of us than the present moment. In fact, many of the characters in these stories have to struggle daily to hold on to a vital sense of the here and now, to ward off memories of pain and loss, of grief and regret in order to simply keep on breathing. The past not only haunts them, it has the power to flood back into consciousness, threatening to wash everything away, mysterious and timeless as the currents that protect the riverbed.

With great delicacy, these stories ask the question: What saves us all from drowning in the past? How do we manage to hold on? Life is a process of becoming, one character reminds us, although only our dreams seem to know where we are headed. Time pours through our hands. Our eyes are open but our hearts are already full to overflowing.

Like the bridges we build, we find solace in the act of telling stories, in making, writing, drawing, and gathering. A child is drowned and a woman releases a poem in a bottle into the river. A man overcomes his past by learning to read and write at the local library – and gets the girl as well! A radio journalist has a surprise for an old woman who was the Tillies Shirt Factory Queen of 1948.

All of these stories display a scrupulous sympathy for the characters and the small rewards they find in their attempts to keep on going. The writing is simple and honest and touched with wonder, like the flickering reflections of the river on the underside of our bridges.

SEAN O'REILLY
Derry, 2010

THE GAP IN THE DOOR

Deirdre could see them both clearly through the gap in the door.

'Saint Conal's!' The boy's voice reverberated off the bare walls and along the corridor towards her.

'Dónal! *Bí ciúin!*'

His father raised his forefinger to his lips. Then, seeing that the boy was crestfallen, Deirdre heard Eoin, her husband, add, 'Your English is coming grand.'

Dónal was fidgeting, his excitement spilling over into nervous energy. Perhaps he'd grown an inch or so since she was admitted. They were both waiting for her on a bench in the passageway. Eoin was teasing him, placing his cap on the boy's head and then removing it again only to ruffle his blond hair with his fingers. Dónal was pretending to box with his father. For Deirdre, it was like seeing daylight again after what seemed an endless season of night.

The world outside sounded turbulent, but with February almost here, the soil would soon breathe again, and the hint of a smile softened her face. Matron was standing behind her, holding the collar of Deirdre's coat agape, guiding her milk-white arms into the hollow sleeves.

'There's a fierce storm building. Button up now, or you'll catch your death,' Matron said.

'I'm weak as water.' Deirdre raised her hand to her brow.

'Come on now, no dillydallying, you've a long train journey ahead of you.'

'Four hours to Burtonport.'

'You're not for stopping over?'

'Maybe Sweeny's Hotel.'

'You'll be for the island in the morning, then?'

3

'The early boat,' Deirdre said. And suddenly the thought of the sheer distance and the shock of the coat's weight gnawed at her confidence. She sighed and sank back down onto the edge of the bed. The tang of bleach rose up from the floor, its strength barely masking the whiff of unemptied commodes.

Nellie Duffy, two beds away, mumbled under the sheets. 'What time do you call this?' she said into the pillow as though it were her dead husband looking back at her. Over the weeks, Deirdre had lost count of the times she had heard her say it.

Directly opposite, Maisie Healy, despite her age, sat upright, bare arms folded tight, drawing her nightdress flat against her sagging breasts, her hips rocking from side to side. And when the bedspring squealed and whistled, she giggled in response like a ten-year-old girl.

'I know what you're thinking, Tommy Gallagher.' Maisie emphasised the words in singsong, then winked. She bit down on her tongue with her gums.

'Don't mind her,' Matron said as she moved to block the possibility of an exchange. 'But it will take a while, you know, before your energy returns. Six weeks takes its toll. Just don't expect too much at the start.' Then she eased Deirdre back up to her feet.

Tuesday would be St Brigid's Day, Deirdre thought. And in advance of the ploughing season, Eoin always turned a sod in the back field, a mark of respect to the saint. Then she imagined Méabh, her eldest, and the twins, Orla and Roisin, making the reed crosses, ready for her return. She smiled.

'Go to your family, but take things easy, mind. Plenty of rest now, don't be afraid to leave things to the girls.'

'I can't say I'm sorry to be going home, but—'

'Go on now. I have your bag and Barney has the trap outside. What with the weather, he won't take no for an answer. He wants to take you down to the station. Your family's waiting. On you go.' Matron ushered Deirdre towards the door, opening it fully.

In the corridor, Deirdre reached out to her left and touched the wall. Her fingers registered where the thicker edge of the olive-green gloss met the start of the cream emulsion. She steadied herself and shivered, huddling under her layer of clothes. When she raised her eyes to take in the scene, the long, narrow space seemed to tilt abruptly. The image of Eoin and Dónal appeared to twist and pull suddenly away from her. She had an awful feeling she was falling through the ceiling, out into the night. A word came whispering into her ear; *Bearna*, she heard, soft as a feather. Overwhelmed, she panicked and closed her eyes.

'Oh, dear God, after all this time,' she cried.

'Deirdre, you're all right, I'm here with you. Breathe slowly.' Matron gripped Deirdre by the elbow.

When Deirdre opened her eyes, everything was normal again. She could see Doctor Eames talking to Eoin. He had his back to her, and as Eoin rose to shake his hand, young Dónal spotted his mother. He came running, his arms wide, his eyes bright with excitement. 'Mam!'

'Dónal, you've sprouted. And wearing brogues, I see,' she said, holding back tears.

'They're Hiúdaí's, but since we're of the same size now ...'

The boy lifted his right knee and presented her his shoe for inspection. Stooping a little, she held his foot in her hand and a memory came back to her of the night she gave birth to him, his tiny feet pulsing new in her palm, and how their softness and warmth had somehow eased her path into sleep.

'Hiúdaí's indeed. Well, you're almost a man now yourself,' she said, composing herself.

Dónal looped an arm around her neck. And as he kissed her, she felt his fingers trace the fresh edge of her greying hair.

'*Do chuid gruaige*, they cut it short,' Dónal declared and stepped back to study his mother more clearly.

'What do you think of your mother, then?' Deirdre asked. Her face flushed as she raised her hand towards her exposed neck.

Dónal looked at the fringe across his mother's forehead and the clean line that ran from just below her ears around the back of her head.

5

'You look younger,' he said.

'I think it's a man's head you have on a boy's shoulders.' Deirdre let out a little laugh. Drawing Dónal to her breast, she breathed in the smell of his head. Then she stood up to face her waiting husband at the end of the corridor. Eoin appeared awkward. He was rotating the rim of his cap through his finger and thumb. In his dark funeral suit, he looked handsome. She sensed his eyes searching for signs of her return to health, longing for the Deirdre he'd married.

'It's good to see you, Eoin. You look well,' the power of her voice seeming to grow as she walked towards him.

'Deirdre,' was all he said as he folded his cap into his pocket and offered her the warmth of his upturned palms. And for a moment she thought they were going to dance.

When they arrived at the station, Barney Bryson declined her gesture of thanks. He simply waved them off, turned the horse and cart around to face the wind and led it back up the hill to the asylum. Tomorrow he would milk the cows and deliver it as usual to Matron. .

Being with her youngest again, Deirdre felt calm. It was a joy to see Dónal so excited by the strange world around him. It was his first time in Letterkenny and only his second time on a train. As they waited for the seven o'clock from Derry, Dónal let go of his mother's hand and wandered off to explore the platform.

'When we land home tomorrow, Méabh will have a roaring fire and a feed of spuds and kippers waiting for us. The girls have been doing a grand job,' Eoin said.

'I'm grateful to you all, really I am. But how will we pay for everything, the medical bills and the train? Surely we can't afford Sweeny's tonight?'

'Paddy the Cope says we've built up a tidy sum of credit, what with the eggs and the fish. And the girls, they've been knitting away. They've sold a woollen each.' He guided her past a trolley-cart piled with luggage and bags of meal. They sat down on a wooden bench. Deirdre leaned into her husband and shivered.

'In his letter, Conor said he's got work down by the Lagán,' she said.

'So he wrote to you? I'm glad to hear that. Sure these days, it's either the Lagán or Scotland. Isn't it better to have him near us?' Eoin reached his arm across her back; he gripped her shoulder, pulled her close and hooked his chin on the crown of her head. 'He'll come visiting before you know it,' he said.

'He sent me young Seán Harkin's memorial card.' Deirdre paused to take a deep breath. 'He was like a brother to Conor.'

'Weren't you like a mother to the two of them?'

'He was only in his twenties,' she sighed.

'Look, love, don't be fretting yourself.'

'And to think but a handful of weeks later all the madness would end,' she said.

'Deirdre, it's the future we need to look to.'

Lifting her head, she turned to face her husband.

'It was such a shock to find Seán hiding under the tarps, and him nearly frozen in his wet clothes. He was so grateful for the bread and soup.'

'You did what you could.'

'If I'd known why he wanted the boat …' Deirdre shook her head.

'Deirdre, you weren't to know there were guns. How could you?'

'But did they have to execute him?'

'He was an Irregular, love. He knew the risks. Honestly, you have to stop torturing yourself. Seán's at peace now. The War is over. We're going home.'

'Thank God Conor's away out of it all. How would we have coped if we'd lost him, too?'

'It's all behind us now. I promise,' Eoin said.

'Before, when I couldn't get Seán out of my head, it was as if he was trying to tell me something. I pictured him standing blindfolded, I heard shots tearing through the mist, I saw his mouth up close, his tongue moving.' Her face contorted as she spoke.

'I know, love, but you're getting better now. Doctor Eames said so. You're only out of hospital. I don't think we should dwell on it. Not now, not for a long while.'

'Eoin, something strange happened tonight, just as I was leaving. I heard Seán's voice. For the first time I actually heard what he said.' She looked directly into her husband's eyes.

'Deirdre, love, Doctor Eames said there could be side effects, what with the treatment and all. But they'll ease with time. He wants you to rest back on Árainn Mór. Wait till the morning, wait till you see our wee home, and us pulling into the harbour at An Leadhb Gharbh. Your heart will lift,' he said. 'Come here to me.' He snuggled her against his chest. 'Myself and the girls now, we're going to take care of you.'

Deirdre could see Dónal standing on top of a suitcase; he was looking at a poster behind framed glass. She could see large yellow lettering with pictures of the landscape within circular frames, one of a beautiful moonlit mountain scene.

'*Cad é a deir sé, cad é a deir sé?*' she heard him say. Then he pointed at the lettering and turned to her.

'It says Donegal Railways, The Land of Tír Chonaill,' said a man who was standing just behind him. 'And that's Barnes Gap. The train's for passing through there tonight,' he added, pointing to the moonlit scene.

As Deirdre listened to the interaction, she began to sense her mood lift. She watched Dónal turn towards the building and spot a series of advertisements printed on metal sheets mounted to the station wall. He pointed to the first one and then looked to the man again.

'Veno's Lightning Cough Cure,' the man said.

Dónal pointed again.

'Ride A Raleigh, The All-Steel Bicycle.'

Dónal pointed again.

'Oxo, Beef in Brief.'

Just then, the sharp whistle of the arriving train startled them and they felt the throb and power of the engine shudder through the platform. Great white plumes of steam funnelled up into the night only for the wind to whip them into the blackness. As if from nowhere, groups of departing passengers appeared. Deirdre rose and pulled Dónal towards her as the large heavy wheels screeched to a halt in front of them. People drifted the length of the platform until they reached the entrance to the carriages. The guard gripped the handles and swung the doors open wide, lifting some of the heavier luggage over the steps and onto the train. When all the passengers and goods were on board, he blew the whistle and the train heaved forward, pulling a freight wagon, three third-class carriages and the guard's van.

Deirdre, Dónal and Eoin entered the first carriage and sat on a long, slatted wooden bench. Dónal settled in between them. The man who had been talking to him took a seat on the bench opposite. He reached forward, lifted something from the bare wooden floor and handed it to Dónal. The boy looked at it and smiled. It was a brass button from a uniform, with a tiny train and the letters L&LSR embossed in the centre.

'A lucky souvenir,' the man said.

'What do you say?' Deirdre asked Dónal.

'*Go raibh maith agat*,' the boy's voice sounded bright in the darkness.

'Neil Doherty,' the man added and reached out in greeting to Deirdre.

'*Cad é mar*? Deirdre and Eoin Bonner, Árainn Mór,' she shook his hand. 'And this is Dónal,' she said, placing her palm on the boy's head.

'Bright as a button,' Neil said and then extended his palm to Eoin and Dónal. The train trundled out west from Letterkenny, along the narrow-gauge line towards Old Town and New Mills. Abruptly, their carriage caught the force of the wind and it rattled loudly and shunted to the left. The oil lamp hanging from the ceiling flickered violently and then struggled back to life again.

'You'll be for no boat in that wind,' came the voice of a red-haired woman sitting a little further along from Neil.

'Lord, no. We're hoping for Sweeny's at Burtonport.' Deirdre wrapped an arm around her son, cuddling him close.

'Well, Creeslough's far enough for Rose McGlinchey,' the red-haired woman said, tapping her chest with her finger.

'It's brewing up a storm,' said Neil.

'It is so,' Deirdre said, a tremor in her voice.

'Kilmacrennan's my stop,' Neil announced. 'But if you'd rather catch the last leg in the morning, you're more than welcome to stay the night with myself and the sister.'

'Oh, no, we couldn't impose,' Deirdre said. 'But thank you.'

'It's not a problem. We're on the main road. The sister takes in a guest now and then, for the Well up at Doon, there. You know, the odd stray pilgrim.'

'A beautiful spot,' Deirdre said.

'That it is,' said Neil.

Then everyone fell silent, lost in thought as the train pushed further into the blackness. After a while, Deirdre tried to focus past her own gaunt reflection in the carriage windows. As the train eased north towards Fox Hall, she strained to read the wind's strength from the sway of the silhouetted tree line. What she saw unsettled her. She looked out and down to her left and caught a glimpse of the wooded grounds of Glebe House and the waters of Lough Gartan. She crossed herself as they passed Saint Columba's birthplace.

The train began to climb and the wind caught the carriage again. As they passed the stop at Church Hill, the lamp purred, then flickered and finally went out. In the sudden black, Dónal clung tightly to his mother.

'Honestly, they never fill them with enough oil,' Rose Mc-Glinchey said.

Eoin reached into his coat and drew out a small brass tube.

'*Cipín*?' Neil offered, handing him a box of matches.

Eoin opened two intricately curved brass doors on the metal cylinder. It revealed a glass chamber housing a white candle. He lifted the brass lid at the top, lit the candle with a match and handed the pocket candle to Dónal.

'*Go raibh maith agat*.' Eoin returned the matches to Neil.

'It's a long way to go in the pitch black in that weather,' Neil sighed.

The trees continued to sway violently out beyond the windows, their trailing branches scratching the carriage; Deirdre felt as though they were trying to claw at her. Dónal shrank low on the bench, nestling against her. She watched as he focused all his attention on the delicate flame in his hands, as if lost in prayer. Neil Doherty drew a pipe to his mouth and thumbed and stoked at it. He struck a match and soon it was glowing red in his fist. His face flickered in the dark. The aroma of the pipe smoke seemed to soothe everyone and the carriage fell silent again.

What with the sound of the wind and the trees, at first Deirdre couldn't be certain. Then she heard it again, clearly: Seán's voice, its tone delicate as a breath in her ear. A shiver ran down her neck and across her shoulders. Something ominous and heavy hit the roof and rolled off into the night.

'Dear God!' she cried, her arm cloaking Dónal.

Crossing a stream, the train swung to the right on its way out towards Kilmacrennan. Deirdre crossed herself again. They braced themselves as the carriages shunted and rattled, the wind getting stronger. The driver slowed to what seemed almost a crawl.

'It's going to be a bad one. You're more than welcome, now,' Neil Doherty said, shifting in his seat and preparing for his stop.

When Deirdre strained to look out again, she saw a landscape strewn with boulders, their lumpy blackness bleak and stark. Up ahead, she imagined the wide valley of the Owencarrow River spreading out below.

Bearna, she heard, its tone urgent in her ear.

'Oh, no!' she called out. This time her voice was panic-stricken.

'Are you all right, Deirdre?' Eoin said, reaching towards her in the dark. And in the silence that followed, he sensed her distress.

'Are you feeling ill?' Neil asked.

'All of a sudden, I feel utterly exhausted. I think I just need to lie down,' she said.

'You know, if Neil can spare us a bed for the night …' Eoin said, squeezing her shoulder.

'I don't like to arrive unannounced,' she said.

'It might be for the best, love.'

'I can't promise a hotel breakfast, but there's porridge and eggs. Catherine, my sister, she'd have it no other way,' Neil Doherty said.

'We wouldn't want something for nothing,' Eoin said.

'Ah, stop it, or I'll offer you the coop,' Neil Doherty chuckled.

'Only if you're sure?' Deirdre asked.

'Sure, didn't I offer?'

'It's just lately I haven't been well,' she added.

'It's settled, then. We'd best be gathering ourselves.' Neil clapped his palms and rubbed them for emphasis as the train came to a halt.

As soon as Deirdre had apologised for the imposition and acknowledged her thanks to Catherine, she'd gone straight into the little bedroom at the gable end of the house. The heavy warmth of the turf fire and the sudden pleasure of privacy had sent her quickly to sleep. But her sleep was fitful and she woke to the sound of crying; distant, at first, then closer, until she realised it was herself who was crying. She had no idea where she was. Her bed was in the wrong place. There was a wall pressing tight against her blanket. She couldn't hear Nellie Duffy or the groans from the others, murmurings she'd gotten used to. Doctor Eames must have locked her in the isolation ward. Confused, she panicked and sat upright. Rapidly she drew the blankets clear of her trembling legs. A hand reached up and gripped her arm, pulling at her, twisting her back towards the pillow. She flung out with her palms, slapping blindly in the dark.

'You're all right, Deirdre, you're all right. It's me – Eoin,' she heard.

She felt an arm wrap around her and recognised Eoin's familiar stubble against her face. Slowly, things began to register again, tumble into place.

'We're in Kilmacrennan, in Catherine and Neil's house. Do you remember now?'

Her body relaxed a little. 'But where's Dónal?'

'He's in the settle, beside the fire. It seemed a shame to lift him,' he said.

'But, Eoin, are we safe?'

'Love, you were crying in your sleep. It was only a dream; you were having a nightmare.'

Suddenly, she was aware of the storm outside. The wind seemed to be prowling around the walls of the house, as though trying to get in. A dog barked, its volume growing, then drifting in the wind.

'I saw everyone falling out through the roof. They were all twisted and contorted. I thought you were all dead.' Deirdre pushed her face into the crook of her husband's neck.

A little later, just as Deirdre began to feel safe, someone banged heavily on the front door of the house. She heard a shout from beyond the threshold, the words indistinct. Then came stirrings from within the house.

'*Fán bomaite*!' came Neil's voice in reply. 'Who is it?' he added.

Deirdre and Eoin scrambled out of bed and began loosely pulling their clothes up over their nightshirts. They heard Neil turn the key and lift the front latch. As the front door opened, the wind rushed like a river into the house, sweeping under the door of their bedroom.

'Doctor Coll!' they heard Neil say.

'Neil, fetch the trap! Hurry! There's been an accident up by the Gap. The Derry train, she's in splinters below the parapet,' the voice said.

Deirdre sank into her husband, the cold air biting her toes, numbing her ankles and feet.

'Mam!' she heard Dónal cry out from beyond the gap in the door.

THE DAY ROOM

When Hannah heard the knock, she recognised its force and rhythm immediately. Seconds later, the impatient face of a nurse thrust itself around the edge of the opened door and into the room.

'Yes, I hear you, Brenda. I'm almost ready,' she said and continued tending to her hair. Hannah held a brush tightly between her frail yet elegant fingers. The brush was from another era. It had a slender gilt handle and an elaborate, floral-framed back. Lying facedown in front of her on the dressing table was a matching hand mirror. Beside the mirror stood a tube of lipstick, its ruby-red tip blunted with use. Next to the lipstick sat a frosted pink powder-dish with a gold-rimmed lid.

'I don't mean to press you, pet. It's just that it's twenty past ten and—'

'Brenda, I'm not your pet. A pet's a budgie, or a cat, or a dog. My name is Hannah. And it's been on my doorplate for over four years now.'

'It's only Radio Foyle, p—, sorry, I mean Hannah. It's not the TV, love.'

'I thought it was the BBC? I'm sure that's what they said. I have it here somewhere. Yes, here it is,' she said, removing a white envelope from her handbag. 'Have you seen my spectacles? Lord knows where I put them. I'm in such a tizzy today.'

'Hannah, Radio Foyle *is* the BBC. The reporter's already here. He's in the day room at the end of the corridor. I think it's only your voice he wants to record. I didn't see any cameras.'

'Radio Foyle? Oh, I see. Is that the same station with … what's his name?'

'Garry Henderson?' Brenda said.

'Oh, no! God forgive me, but that's one man I can't stomach. He can be very crude, you know, vulgar at times. No, not him. It's the other fella, the nice one: Seamus. Aye, Seamus Doyle, that's his name. Now, he's a lovely-looking man.'

'Yes, Hannah, that's the one. But it's not him. It's some young fella.'

'Well, why didn't they tell me it was the wireless? For heaven's sake!'

'Now, don't be fussin' yourself. Honestly, Hannah. Really, you look grand. You'll be fine.'

Hannah turned slightly in her chair so that she was facing Brenda.

'Well, don't just stand there. Help me up. Let's not keep him waiting,' she said, offering Brenda her left forearm.

When Hannah entered the day room, she saw a man in his late twenties flipping through a dog-eared copy of the *Reader's Digest*. What looked like a black microphone lay on the table in front of him. He stood up to greet her and she saw that he was tall and had the most beautiful brown eyes. His dark hair was cropped short and groomed. It had a sort of tussled appearance.

'Hello. Excuse me a moment,' she said to the reporter, her attention focused on her armchair, the one she always sat on. Everyone had their own little spot in the day room, and as usual her chair was positioned beside the window. She did like a window seat. From there she could watch the world go by. The light would be on her best side.

'Brenda, the chair, it's facing the wrong way,' she said.

'Oh, sorry. You want to face the river? Are you sure now? There's nothing to look at but them oul' fuel tanks and the builder's yard. Do you not want to look out at the rhododendrons? Sure aren't they all in bloom?'

'I want to see God's daylight. Get the sun on my face. I'm not dead yet, you know.' Hannah turned and winked at the young man.

'Don't be saying that now, Hannah. You'll not be leaving us for a few years yet,' Brenda said.

The young reporter helped reposition the chair and Brenda slowly eased Hannah into the seat. Then she raised Hannah's feet onto a small footstool and placed a tartan blanket on her lap.

'Now, Hannah, are you warm enough?' Brenda asked.

'It's very stuffy in here. Could you open the window a bit and let in some fresh air?' Hannah replied.

'Would you like a wee cup of tea and a biscuit?' Brenda opened the window slightly.

'Yes. But don't be giving me one of those bloody mugs. Excuse my language, son. But God help us, them's good for nothing but soaking false teeth. I'd like a proper cup; you know, one with a saucer. If you're stuck, you can borrow some china from my room. What about yourself, son? Would you like a drop of tea?'

'Aye, a coffee would be nice.'

'I can make you a cappuccino if you like?' Brenda said.

'That'd be grand.'

'Oh, they've everything here at Oak Manor. It's like a proper five-star hotel. No wallpaper, though, everything's emulsion. Magnolia, for heaven's sake.' Hannah gestured at the walls. 'A handsome face like yours brightens the place up,' she added, smiling at the reporter.

'Watch yourself with that one. I hope you're married?' Brenda joked.

'Ah, now, a man as good-looking as you, I'm sure you have a sweetheart, son,' Hannah said to the young man.

'Should I put this on the door now, or can it wait for the tea?' Brenda flashed the 'Do Not Disturb' sign at the two of them.

'Brenda, will you stop now? You're embarrassing the poor fella.'

'I'm sorry to disappoint you, ladies, but you're too late, I'm well spoken for. Ciaran, my partner, and I, we've been together for four years now,' the reporter explained.

'Oh, isn't that lovely. Well, I'll not hold you up any longer. I'll go and get your drinks.' Brenda left swiftly, closing the door behind her.

Hannah glanced at the reporter and offered him a subtle smile. He returned the gesture.

'That gave her a gunk. Good for you, son. I hope you're both very happy together. She's a real busybody, that one. Means well, but God forgive me, there are days when I could see her far enough.' Hannah lifted her eyebrows.

The reporter dragged his seat closer to Hannah. When he was directly facing her, he smiled and reached out to shake her hand.

'Hello, Mrs Jordan. My name's Jonathan Maxwell.'

'Well, I'm sorry to say, Jonathan, it's just plain Miss Jordan. No-one would have me, son, even though I was the nineteen forty-eight Tillies Queen. You know, Tillie and Henderson's, the shirt factory?' And with the fingers of both hands, Hannah fluffed the white bloom of hair behind her ears.

'You'd think they'd have snapped me up. My friend Ruby used to say that if you're a looker, it can sometimes scare men off,' she chuckled.

'Is it okay if I call you Hannah?'

'Of course. There're no airs and graces about me. Sure aren't I from Abercorn Road, for heaven's sake!'

When the tea and coffee arrived, they sat for a while and sipped their drinks. Now and then, Hannah looked out wistfully, beyond the builder's yard, towards the old naval dock. It lay abandoned behind a heap of broken tarmac on a plot of waste ground next to Sainsbury's. When she finished her tea, she handed Jonathan the cup, a half-eaten biscuit still resting on the saucer. The cup rattled gently as he placed it on the table. A red kiss of lipstick glistened on its fine porcelain rim.

'I prefer a Jammie Dodger, myself. I was never that fussed on Digestives. Pardon me for saying so, but they give me wind. Of course, if they're Chocolate Digestives, I could eat the packet, but only if it's dark chocolate. I love a bit of dark chocolate,' she said, smiling softly.

'Chocolate gives me a headache,' Jonathan said.

'Ah, well, that's a pity. Still, I'm sure being in love is sweet enough?'

'Do you mind if I start recording, Hannah?'

'Oh, sorry, son. Never mind me. Yes, I'm ready.'

'So just to remind you. As we said in the letter, the theme of the programme is Derry during World War II. It would be great if you could say something about working in the shirt factory or talk about your memories of the war. Don't worry about the order. We'll edit the recording back at the station.'

'So I'll not be on the wireless today?' Hannah's voice carried a mixture of disappointment and relief.

'No. Your piece today will be part of a series called Under the Apple Tree. As far as I know, it's scheduled for broadcast this coming autumn. Then, after it's been on air, they'll pop it on to the website as a podcast. Anyone in the world can hear it then.'

'Oh, dear God, it all seems very complicated.'

'Don't worry, Hannah. Think of it as if it's just you and me. Imagine we're having a wee chat. Try to forget about the listeners.'

'Well, I suppose I could manage that. That sounds easier.'

'I'm switching the mic on now. So whenever you're ready, just talk away. You'll be grand.'

'Well now, let me see. I could talk about the song, you know, *Under The Apple Tree*?'

'That sounds like a good place to start.'

'I'd say it was nineteen forty-two. No, I'm telling a lie, it was probably nineteen forty-three when I first heard *Under The Apple Tree*. Ruby Dobson, my best friend, worked in the same section as me in Tillies. We were both front-stitchers. Anyhow, we used to meet up after work regular. And one night we went to see the picture *Private Buckaroo* in Saint Columb's Hall. Oh, it was such a funny film. We were laughing and kee-hoing all the way through. There's the bit when the three Andrews Sisters pull this big apple tree onto the stage. It's so long ago now, but from memory, I mind it was a painting of a tree on a big board. It was on casters. And as soon as they had the tree right behind them, the three of them started singing. Well, we all joined in, of course. How did it go now?'

Hannah gathered her thoughts for a moment and then, with her voice shaking, she sang.

Don't sit under the apple tree with anyone else but me,
Anyone else but me, anyone else but me.
No! No! No!
Don't sit under the apple tree with anyone else but me,
Till I come marchin' home.

When she finished singing, her face brightened and she laughed gently, as if surprised by the sound of her own voice. Then she eased a crumpled paper-handkerchief from under her sleeve and dabbed the edges of her mouth.

'It's my dentures, son, they're new,' she said and then continued. 'When the Andrews Sisters finished singing, all of a sudden, the picture stopped and the announcement came up on the screen. Then the air-raid sirens went off. Oh, dear God, it was pandemonium. People were scrambling over the seats. And do you know what? It was such a wild silly thing to do. But Ruby and myself, we just sat there in the dark. We prayed to the good Lord that he would spare us. Eventually, when the all-clear came, the picture started up again. We were the only two people left in the hall. Well, we just sat there and we enjoyed ourselves.'

'So life went on as normal, then?'

'Well, it had to. The war made things difficult, of course. During the blackout, the buses had black discs over the headlamps to weaken the lights. I mind one of the bus conductors: he had a leather strap around his neck with a bicycle lamp clipped to it. It was the only way for him to see the tickets and the money. Sometimes in the dark you'd get confused, though. I got off the bus once at the top of Rock Road. Can you believe it? I thought I was at Clarendon Street.

'But like everything, you got used to it. During an air raid, we had to walk out to Bridgend, throngs of men, women and wee'uns, in the pitch black. It got that I began to recognise people by their shape in the dark. You know, the way they stood, or even the sound of their footsteps might be enough. One night, we even walked out as far as Burt. I remember looking down over the farms there at the edge of the Swilly. The land is so flat. The Donegal fellas had placed all their tractors and trailers out on the fields in case the German planes tried to land. All the machinery was shimmering in the drizzle under the moonlight. I was soaked through. But I didn't care. It just looked so pretty, you know, ghostly.'

'It must have been tough at times?'

'Oh, it was. There was that terrible explosion at Messines Park. The bombs came down on parachutes, you see. I'm not certain of the year now, but I mind it was a bitter cold Easter night. One of the rescuers came stumbling out of the rubble holding a wee'un in his arms. When Ruby and myself went over to help, the man said he found her cradled between her dead parents. I looked at her wee face covered in dust, and didn't she sneeze. It's clear as a picture in my mind, the cloud of her breath and her waking back into life.'

'A survivor.'

'That she was.'

'I'm sure there was a bit of mischief, too?'

'Oh, we had some laughs, all right. There was the smuggling between Derry and Donegal. If I wanted a new pair of shoes, all I had to do was take the train over to Buncrana. I'd put my new shoes on and throw away my old ones. My cousins in Inishowen, they used to give me eggs. You see, you weren't allowed to bring eggs across into Derry, not if they where in their shells. But you could bring any amount of eggs in jars. I used to bake cakes with them. Sometimes I'd swap a wee flan for a packet of cigarettes from the Navy, out along by the quay there. Just like in the films. I'd let the smoke curl up past my face, like a blue ribbon. If I was really lucky, I might get a pair of stockings. Ruby used to say to me, "Hannah, dear," she'd say, "you've a quare leg for a button boot." Oh, I used to laugh. I'd imagine I was Lauren Bacall.'

Hannah's gaze drifted again, out towards the old dock. It was as if she were watching something only she could see, beyond the tumble of waste ground.

'Ah, she was a real character was our Ruby. She's gone now, gone to her maker. But then, they're all gone now, except me, and a couple of old stragglers. I'll tell you a secret: I still dream that there'll be a man waiting for me, you know, on the other side, like Humphrey Bogart,' Hannah chuckled. 'I don't suppose you believe in heaven yourself, son?'

'It would be nice to, Hannah. But nah, I can't say I do. But you were saying, you and Ruby, you both worked in the factory, right through the war?'

'We did indeed. Tillies, now they were strict. You had to be at the factory on time. Once the door was closed, you wouldn't get in. I mind many times I was running late. You'd be dashing up the iron steps, or across the wooden gangway. And there, standing at the top with his hand on the door bars, was Harry Morgan. Once the factory horn stopped and there was a gap in the line of girls, he'd just slam the door shut.

'You see, in Tillies during the war years, we had to make military uniforms, so we were wild busy. It was hard work, but we kept ourselves amused. We had some laughs, though, the girls, Ruby and myself. You know, we used to put little notes into the breast pocket of the shirts. It was just a wee bit of fun. Whoever got your shirt got your wee note, you see. What was it now? Ah, dear, I can't mind it now. But we put our addresses on the back. It was all so innocent, you know.'

* * *

It had been almost six months since the radio broadcast. The nurses teased Hannah, saying she had become a celebrity now.

Her singing had impressed everyone. And sometimes after a sherry, she'd sing a verse or two. They liked that.

Today, sitting in the day room, Hannah was very excited. Jonathan was coming to visit her again. He would be arriving any minute now and he was bringing someone with him. Her heart was racing when she looked up and saw both men enter the room. Jonathan was a little plumper, she thought. And his friend, well, she guessed, mid-fifties perhaps. He was balding, appeared good-natured, though. They were both smiling.

'You're looking well, Hannah. It's nice to see you again,' Jonathan said, leaning forward and kissing her on the cheek.

'And it's nice to see you, too, Jonathan,' she replied, clearly basking in the attention. 'Is this Ciaran, your partner?' she asked, gesturing to the older man.

'Oh, no. Sorry, Hannah, I'd like you to meet Robert Cook.'

'Oh, pardon me. Hello, Robert,' Hannah held out her hand.

'It's a pleasure,' Robert said, holding her fingers briefly. And with that, both men sat down in front of her.

'How have you been keeping?' Jonathan asked.

'Oh, I'm grand. The days can be long, though, especially with winter on its way.'

'Do you remember I told you we'd broadcast our radio programme during the autumn?' Jonathan said.

'Sure didn't we have the wireless on here in the day room? It was a Saturday afternoon if I remember right. We had lots of tea and cake. It was all very nice, you know, listening to all the different stories. It brought it all back. Although, hearing my own voice, now that was strange.' She relaxed into her chair and smiled.

Just then, Brenda popped her head around the door.

'Did I hear someone mention Hannah's voice? Now, don't you believe it boys, this one's a natural. Sings like a proper nightingale; if she gets a wee tipple to whet her whistle, sure aren't we all ears? She could win the *X Factor*, that one,' Brenda declared.

'Ah, now, don't be exaggerating,' Hannah protested, her face collapsing into a chuckle.

'Tea, coffee, anyone?' Brenda asked.

'Would you have such a thing as a sherry glass?' Jonathan asked as he produced a bottle from his shoulder bag.

'Oh, celebrations,' Brenda winked at Hannah. 'Three sherry glasses coming up,' she said and left.

'Is it not too early?' Robert Cook asked.

'At my age, Robert, nothing is too early. Well, this is a nice surprise,' she said, her eyes fixed on the bottle.

'Do you remember I said we'd pop your recording onto the BBC website?' Jonathan said.

'I think so. All that newfangled stuff now, I don't understand it. But I mind you mentioned something.'

'Once it's on the web, anyone in the world can listen to it on a computer, from as far away as Australia or North America,' Jonathan added.

'Now, isn't that something?' she mused.

'Robert here heard your broadcast in Canada.'

'Goodness, you've come a long way,' she said.

'I'm over visiting family. My parents emigrated in the fifties,' Robert replied.

'Isn't that nice. Do you know, I'm overwhelmed. But it's lovely to know that other people were listening.'

'That's just it, I was. And when I heard your name, it immediately rang a bell,' Robert said.

'But how would you know my name?' Hannah shook her head in disbelief.

'Because of this.' Robert withdrew something from his jacket pocket. 'I found it in my uncle's belongings. It was in among all sorts of knick-knacks, untouched for years. He was in the Royal Navy. Sadly, he died in the Battle of Dieppe in World War Two.' Robert held out a small envelope to Hannah.

'Thank you,' she said, accepting it. 'Just a minute now, I'll need my spectacles.'

Hannah opened a burgundy-coloured case and withdrew her glasses, wiping them carefully on the little cloth. She eased them onto her face, adjusting them along her nose until they were comfortably in place. She raised the envelope up towards her face for closer inspection.

'Let's see now.' She examined it carefully. Then her eyebrows lifted in surprise. 'Lord save us! It's addressed to me. How can that be? It clearly says *Hannah Jordan, forty-two Abercorn Road, Derry*. I don't understand. That's me!'

'Perhaps you should open it?' Robert said.

'It's never been opened before?'

'It would appear not.'

Hannah lifted the envelope up to the light of the window, her hand trembling with anticipation.

'Well, there's definitely something inside,' she said.

'Why don't you open it?' Robert urged her.

'It's such a precious thing. You know, maybe I shouldn't.'

'Go on, open it,' Robert insisted.

Emboldened, she placed the envelope on her blanketed lap, easing the sealed paper tongue away from the back. The glue was dry and brittle and it parted without difficulty. Peeking inside, she found a scrap of folded yellowing notepaper. She withdrew it, opening it flat so she could read the writing.

'The ink is almost gone,' she said.

'What does it say?' Robert and Jonathan asked in unison.

'My name and address are on the back. That's my writing. Would you believe it? That's one of the wee notes that I slipped into the uniforms in Tillies!' Hannah leaned back into her seat. She exhaled audibly and shook her head gently. 'Who would have thought, after all these years?'

'Is there anything else?' Robert asked.

'Wait till we see now.' She took a second peek. 'Indeed there is,' she said, sliding a small black-and-white photograph out onto her palm. 'Is that him?' Hannah tilted the photograph towards Robert.

'Yip. That's my uncle,' Robert said.

'His name is on the back. Albert Miller? Isn't that nice? And look, he's written, *If you're single, drop me a line.*'

She turned the front of the photograph around to savour the face of the young man smiling out at her. He was standing in bright sunlight, dressed in a Navy uniform; his short hair parted to one side. There was a cheeky quality to his gaze, she thought.

'He's very handsome! I could just picture him in a film!'

There was a knock at the door. It opened and Brenda entered, carrying a tray of sherry glasses.

* * *

Hannah loved the smell of freshly cleaned cotton; it was always somehow comforting and the softness against her skin was cosy. She was wearing her nightdress, the one with tiny blue flowers on it, forget-me-nots. Tonight she had picked it out especially. There was a small, embroidered breast pocket, mainly for decoration. But tonight it would have its uses.

As she sat looking at herself in the mirror, the gentle glow from the three sherries she had allowed herself with Jonathan and Robert brought a smile to her face. She hummed quietly as she finished tending to her hair. Setting the brush back down on the dressing table, she closed the lid of her night cream and checked that everything was in its proper place for the morning. The envelope that Robert had given her was propped against the frosted-pink powder-dish. Her fingers trembled slightly as she teased out the photograph of Albert Miller. And for a few moments she took in his young smile. Then she slipped the weathered print carefully into the breast pocket of her nightgown. She rose, turned towards her bed, and was about to page the nurse. But no, she decided, tonight she would climb in all by herself.

BIRTHMARK

In the dream, Fergus is back in Richmond Crescent, his childhood home. He's kneeling on a sheepskin rug in front of a coal fire. To the left of the chimneybreast in the corner of the room stands a walnut china cabinet. It has two glass shelves. Long mirror tiles forming a back panel give the illusion that there are six figurines on the first shelf, eight crystal glasses on the second and two rubber bullets on the base. He is staring at his mother's reflection in the glass door. A birthmark maps one side of her face, like spilt wine. A purple rose, he calls it to lift her mood. A hairline crack in the curved door pane bisects her image distorting her face, making her smile look crooked. Even so, as his mother sits on the sofa behind him, Fergus can see that she's crying again.

'Ma, what's wrong?' he says and turns towards her.

Fergus wakes. This time the fever has been prolonged, but his abdominal pain has gone. His mouth tastes sour. Sweat still lingers cold in his clothes. Raising his left hand, he stares at his fingerprints, heightened by smudges of charcoal. They are trembling. His index finger is held in the grip of a small clamp. A grey flex trails from the plastic clip leading to a display of pulsing red numbers. Raising himself up, he sits, dangling his legs over the edge of the bed. Then he tilts his head, first to the left, and then to the right, as though the action is somehow sifting his thoughts.

'Mr McLaughlin? Mr Fergus McLaughlin?' he hears as a curtained screen is pulled sharply to one side. Fergus gives a slight jolt.

'I'm your man,' he says. Suddenly aware of his swinging legs, he stills them. A balding doctor wearing designer glasses and a long white coat stands in front of him. Beside him stands some fresh-faced guy dressed in a cream shirt and striped tie. Learning the ropes, Fergus guesses. Finally, his attention rests on the soft eyes of a nurse in a dark-blue uniform. 'This is Mr Steele, your consultant,' she says, referring to the older man.

'How's the form?' Fergus replies.

'Mr McLaughlin, given your test results, I'd like to keep you in overnight, just for observation. Grace will make the arrangements,' Steele says, gesturing to the nurse. 'But firstly, I have a few questions, if that's okay with you?' he adds.

'Sure, fire away.' Fergus shrugs.

'Date of birth, June fifteenth, sixty-seven. That correct?' Steele asks, reading from notes.

'Aye, same day as Noddy Holder. *Goodbye To Jane*,' Fergus offers and, eliciting no response, he adds, 'Slade; you know, the seventies glam-rock band?'

Steele ignores the comment. The younger man and Grace manage embarrassed smiles.

'So, at thirty, if we say you've been drinking since your late teens, that makes twelve years,' Steele says.

'Add another five.'

'You started drinking at thirteen?' Steele lifts his eyes from his notes and peeks over the rim of his glasses.

'Old English Cider. You know, cheap and cheerful,' Fergus says. 'Although I wouldn't touch the stuff now. Too sweet; gives me a thumping hangover. Nah, it's stout and a chaser for me.'

'So, in a typical week, how many units would you drink?' asks the younger man.

'Units?' Fergus makes an exaggerated frown. 'You mean pints?'

'Not quite,' Steele interrupts. 'Grace, would you mind?'

The nurse hands Fergus a leaflet. It opens into a chart, the days of the week in a column on the left and a row of drinking glasses across the top. The words 'Beer, Wine, Spirits, Cocktail and Other' differentiate the graphic symbols above a column of boxes aligned with the days of the week.

'Forms. Where would we be without them?' Fergus jokes.

'Have a wee read and just pop a number in the boxes,' Grace says.

The younger man removes a biro from his pocket and offers it to Fergus. 'It's important to be honest. There's no point in tweaking the figures.' He raises his eyebrows for emphasis.

'Can you imagine me sipping cocktails?' Fergus mimes the stem of a glass between his index finger and thumb, his smallest finger raised at an exaggerated angle. He tilts his head, mocking a pose.

'Mr McLaughlin, you have an enlarged pancreas. It can be a life-threatening condition and, as you've discovered, extremely painful. Alcohol is often a contributing factor in pancreatic disease. I would strongly recommend you refrain, temporarily, if not completely. Does that pose a problem?' Steele says.

Fergus glances at the chart. 'Nah. Not a bother.'

* * *

Lit by the afternoon sun, a naked ebony body is curled forward on the floor. Odette's buttocks are positioned in front of an easel with her spine arcing forward into the room. None of her limbs are visible. The impression is of an enormous pear. Fergus is making wide, sweeping gestures on a canvas as tall as a door, his energy flowing down his arm, along his fingers and out through the charcoal. What emerges on the surface, although abstract, is a brooding human seedpod. On an armchair to his left, the weekend paper lies open revealing an illustrated review of his work. He smiles, recalling the lines: 'McLaughlin captures embryonic form with the monumental presence of bronze. His drawings seem to eroticise life, alluding simultaneously to the act of dying and, increasingly in his new work, to the process of becoming.'

Fergus's thoughts drift back to Suzi, a teenage girlfriend. She had felt no shame in posing nude. And gradually he had learned to capture the language of her body, to craft meaning in his depiction of her form. The dark pattern of her childhood had left its marks on her limbs. But she had been emphatic.

'Don't hide them,' she had said. And through his images of Suzi he came to understand: his drawing was an act of witness.

Fergus's eye is drawn to a sudden flare of light on the mantelshelf. Like a prism, a glass cube casts a ribbon of purple obliquely across a small, unframed portrait of Odette. The loose sketch is casually propped behind a transparent trophy. The words 'Best Documentary – Foyle Film Festival 1998' are etched on the crystal surface. They shimmer and spangle in the light.

'Trauma,' he says. 'Strange how it feeds the imagination.'

'Sorry?' Odette's voice is muffled against the floorboards.

'Even your bloody award illuminates my work,' he adds.

'Fergus, what *are* you on about?'

'Your film. I bet you never dreamed your fucked-up childhood would drag you to Ireland, win you a prize in the Maiden City.'

'That's not why I accepted it. You know that, Fergus,' she says. 'It's for all those lives that go unnoticed back home. I'm proud of my LA neighbourhood.'

'You almost dropped the bloody thing when I made the presentation.'

'I was nervous. We're not all like you, Fergus. We don't all wear masks.'

Standing at his easel in Pump Street with Odette posing in front of him, Fergus recalls how barely a month after that first meeting they woke to the rhythm of rain on the skylight. And she told him then how she missed the California sun. 'The sound of cicadas is punctuating my dreams,' she said. Unusually, for Fergus, their bond was strong. Six months was a record. Somehow their relationship was special; he was beginning to understand that. Or maybe he just recognised himself in the kids that Odette had caught on film. He tried not to think of her leaving.

'I'm getting a cramp. Can we take a break?' Odette calls out, her voice sounding tired.

'Sure.'

Still with her back to him, Odette stands upright, stretches slowly and then assumes her favourite yoga posture.

A body warmer hangs from a bolt on the easel and Fergus slips his hand into a pocket and removes a small bottle of Bush. Unscrewing the cap, he takes a generous swig.

When Odette finishes her brief routine, she unclasps a tortoiseshell hairclip and her dark, beaded locks fall casually about her neck and shoulders. Turning to face him, her mouth drops open in shock.

'Oh … my … God,' she emphasises each word. 'What did Steele tell you in December?'

'It's only a qu—'

'You're seriously ill!'

'Relax, will you?'

'How can I? You've become a goddamn Irish cliché. Can't you see that?'

'That's a joke, coming from a naked African-American "saluting the fucking sun" or whatever it's called.'

'Oh, I see. You think I'm a joke, do you?'

'That's not what I meant.'

'How dare you! You're the Irish drunk, slugging whiskey at three o'clock in the afternoon.'

'Jesus, Odette, give me a bloody break.'

'I'm shivering here, for you and your art. And all you can do is drink, literally behind my back. Look at it, the bottle's practically empty. My God, Fergus, you agreed.'

'It's only a quarter bottle, for fuck's sake.'

'Fergus, I'm not taking this shit. I know this script. I wrote it.' Odette flings the hairclasp at his feet and strides off, slamming the door behind her. The clasp bounces a few times, then rolls onto one side and rocks gently. The sound of the door, like a gunshot, reverberates in the room. Fergus stares at the floor until the clasp is motionless.

Suddenly, he's in the kitchen of 13 Richmond Crescent. It's the summer of 1979. A Tupperware bowl tumbles to the floor, spins, rocks, then settles motionless at his feet; the apples it held scatter across the tiny scullery. His mother is shouting,

'Jesus, Mary and Joseph! Fergus, get down! Get down!' Then more shots ring out. His pet dog, Bran, barks in the back lane. Somewhere behind the house, a sniper is firing at a foot-patrol returning to Fort George Military Base. His mother is curled forward in a foetal position on the floor. Her arms, initially gesturing, are now hidden beneath her. Her buttocks are directly in front of him. The rest of her body fades into the shadows. Fergus slumps behind her to the sound of someone shouting, in an English accent, 'Back of number thirteen'. The sniper runs off. Moments later, Fergus hears footsteps thundering in pursuit, up the back lane, then bottlenecking in his backyard. Bran's barking becomes frenzied. The gunfire is louder now, more powerful. Despite being twelve years old, he recognises the four shots are from an SLR. Then silence. Fergus has forgotten to breathe. He lets out a chestful of air. Bran is dead; he knows that now. A cassette player dangles by its flex from the table. His mother is sobbing uncontrollably into the space between her body and the lino. Reaching out to comfort her, he sees that all his fingers are shaking. Suddenly, he realises that he has wet himself. Ashamed, he withdraws his hand. Soldiers kick in the back door.

Fergus swallows the last mouthful of Bush as a burn of pain returns. He remembers how his mother remained hysterical long after the raid that day. And later, when the ambulance took her away, across the river to Gransha, he'd drifted between his Uncle Bobby and his friend Tony's house. For the first few months, he'd made trips to the Kesh. But after a while, he'd stopped visiting his father in prison. He felt stupid, the two of them just sitting there staring across the divide. He didn't know him that well, what with his father being active and on the run for so long. What was he supposed to say anyway?

'Do you like the roses, Ma?' Fergus had said, pointing to the vase the day she came home. But he could tell she wasn't fully there, not really. It felt as if she was all used up, like something discarded, a dead leaf caught by a current, drifting further and further away. He should have held her that day in the scullery.

'You were only a boy, Fergus! Who comforted *you*?' Odette had said when she challenged him only last month. She was right. He could see that. But no matter how often he chewed over the same scene, he regretted not reaching out, not putting his arm around her.

Fergus picks up the portrait of Odette from the mantelshelf and with the stub of charcoal writes something along the bottom. Odette is here now, with me, he tells himself. He leaves the studio and walks to their bedroom. Opening the door gently, he sees her sleeping figure partly covered by the duvet. She's wearing her ankle-length cotton dress, the one she wore when they first met. Walking towards the bed, he wants to reach out, to hold her. But instead, he sets the A4 sketch on the table, just below her lamp. She'll find it in the morning when she wakes. Silently, he walks around to his side of the bed and lowers himself onto the edge of the mattress.

'Today's my ma's anniversary, for fuck's sake,' he whispers to the room. Without removing his clothes, he swivels his legs onto the bed, lies back heavily and closes his eyes. Within minutes, he sinks into sleep.

Although the entire city seems to be dreaming, Fergus feels wide awake. His skin is clammy and he decides to splash his face under the bathroom tap. Rising, he glances down at Odette. She's beautiful, he thinks, and for a moment he considers how lucky he is. Then he crosses the threshold.

Everything appears fresh and vivid as the water trickles through his fingers, cooling his skin. By the light of the mirror-cabinet, he sprinkles his forehead and takes in his own distorted reflection. Despite the hairline crack in the glass, he looks healthy for a change, peaceful even. But gradually he becomes aware of something niggling him. He can barely hear it. It sounds like sobbing, then he realises it's coming from the bedroom. In the mirror, he sees Odette huddled on the floor.

She keeps lifting her head, as if searching for a star in the night sky. She's crying, crying sorely.

'Odette, what's wrong?' he calls. Then turning towards her, he realises she's cradling someone. His gaze lifts to the face, only to discover that he is looking back at himself.

* * *

A wiry, white mongrel with a patch of red covering one half of its face limps as it passes Badger's Pub. It crosses Newmarket Street, chasing a dove up the sandstone steps of St Columb's Hall. The dove flaps off, then settles on a windowsill, casting a shadow onto the floor inside. The room inside is a gallery and a mulatto boy of about ten steps eagerly into the frame of light. He points at a small, framed portrait on the wall, his index finger charged with excitement.

'Mom, it's you!' he shouts and looks for her among the throng of people. 'This one is you, isn't it?' he repeats, rocking on his heels.

A woman approaches, her beaded hair held loosely by a clasp. She embraces the boy.

'So I look ten years younger?' She draws him up on to his toes and kisses his temple.

'Well, kind of,' he says and looks again at the portrait.

His mother laughs and tussles with him playfully. 'I see.'

'I'm only joking, Mom.' He twists as she tickles him.

'Is that so?' she says and relents. Then she points to a white label on the wall next to the frame. 'Would you like to read this for me?'

'Only if you promise not to tickle me.'

'It's a deal. Now, take your time, Fergus.'

The boy leans towards the gallery wall for a closer look at the label. 'My Purple Rose – Charcoal on Paper – Fergus McLaughlin – Nineteen ninety-eight,' he says loudly to his mother and the room.

DANCING THE POLKA

Francie Boyle had just dozed off when the sound of his letterbox snapping shut woke him with a start. Through the Venetian blinds of his lounge, he glimpsed the postman skip over the low wall running between his and the McMonagles' front gardens. And as the mail dropped through his neighbour's door, the postman started whistling the first few bars of *See Me Dance The Polka*.

Ever since Francie was a boy, the tune gave him the jitters. An image would pop into his head of Spencer Tracy wearing an evil grin. Then he'd hear a deranged laugh echoing down the years from the movie *Dr Jekyll and Mr Hyde*. And Spencer Tracy would open a creaking door in Francie's memory onto the foreboding streets of Victorian London.

Francie let the wave of a childhood shiver wash over him, rubbed his face with his hands, scratched the bridge of his nose and yawned. Friday's edition of the *Derry Journal*, open at the sports section, slipped from his lap as he rose from the armchair. When he entered the hallway, sure enough, there was mail waiting for him in a loose pile on the doormat. He stooped and sifted through a mix of the usual supermarket flyers and vouchers from some garden centre until he uncovered a letter. He liked getting mail. But today was different. Maybe it was just waking up to the sound of the whistling postman. But somehow he didn't have a good feeling as he picked up the white envelope. Francie flipped it over in his hands. When he recognised the red frank on the top right-hand corner, a relieved smile spread across his face.

'Yes! Ninety quid!' he said and punched the air in the sunlit hallway. Another short story published, he thought, earning him a handy wee top-up to his pension. Eagerly tearing open the envelope, he pulled out a folded A4 letter. He squinted in frustration until he lowered his glasses back down onto his nose. Through the dust of his varifocals, he could see it wasn't a cheque after all. And as he read the letter, it began to tremble in his hand. He was stunned at first, then worried and then 'Catastrophe!' was all he said.

* * *

'I don't get it,' Barney said. 'Surely it's good news?' he added, admiring the creamy top of his cappuccino. Then he scooped a dollop of the warm froth from the rim and spooned it into his mouth and smiled. 'Dear God, you can't beat a nice big generous cappuccino dusted with cinnamon. You know, I think she fancies me, that one. Look, do you see the wee powdery heart she put on the top?' said Barney, nodding in the direction of the waitress who served him.

'Speaking of hearts, that stuff'll clog your arteries,' Francie said.

'Who cares? Sure after sixty years, isn't the damage done? Anyway, there's still life left in the old dog yet.' Barney smiled as the waitress approached a table nearby and began clearing away the cups and plates.

When she returned to the service counter, Francie raised his eyebrows and sighed. 'I take it you've noticed she's half your age. Let's face it, Barney, we're both too old for love now. Well past our sell-by date.'

'Coming from a man with a dark, dirty secret, that's a bit rich.' Barney forced a grin. Then, seeing that Francie was truly downhearted, he added, 'Does nobody else ... I mean, surely I'm not the only one who knows you write?'

Francie looked straight at Barney and nodded. 'I use a *nom de plume*.'

'A what?'

'It's French. I use a pen name.'

'Oh, I see. Nice one, very sophisticated.'

Francie looked decidedly preoccupied. 'As soon as I read

the letter, the first thing I thought of was Beckett,' he said.

'The footballer?' Barney asked.

'No, not Beckham, you eejit. Beckett! Samuel Beckett. You know, the Irish writer. "Catastrophe!", that's what he said when he heard he'd won the Nobel.'

'But I thought that was Famous Seamus?'

'Aye, but before that. Jeez, Barney, do you not know nothin'?'

'Listen, we can't all be Albert-bloody-Einstein, you know.' Barney feigned a wounded expression.

'I'm sorry, Barney, but what am I goin' to do? I didn't sleep a wink last night. Here, take this. I can't stomach it. My nerves are playing up.' He shoved an oversized blueberry muffin towards Barney.

'Happy days.' Reaching for Francie's fork, he added. 'You didn't put this in your gob, did you?'

'My God! Haven't we only just sat down? It's as clean as a flamin' whistle.'

Barney dropped the fork on the floor. Just then, the waitress was delivering a salad roll to a table near the door; as she passed, she picked up the fork.

'It's okay. You stay where you are, dear. I'll bring you a fresh one,' she said and headed back to the counter.

'You did that on purpose,' Francie said when she was out of earshot.

'No, I didn't.'

'Yes, you did. Honestly, what are you like!' Francie let out a sigh.

When the woman returned, she handed Barney a saucer with a fork wrapped in a red paper napkin. A courtesy gold square of dark chocolate sat beside it.

'There you are now. Enjoy your muffin,' she said.

'Thanks, love. You're a proper Cinderella,' Barney said.

'Just doin' my job, dear,' she beamed and returned to the service till.

'God, you're so old-fashioned. Nobody says "love" anymore. It's not PC,' Francie scolded.

'Well, I think they should. Not enough love in the world if you ask me. Anyway, you should know,' Barney chuckled. Then he unwrapped the gold foil and popped the chocolate into his mouth. 'Mmm, yummy. First a cinnamon heart, then dark chocolate. I wonder what's next? Maybe I should ask her out. What do you think?'

'Oh, God!' Francie dropped his forehead into his hands and stared blankly at the tabletop.

'I really don't get what all the fuss is about. It's the Buncrana Library, for God's sake. It's hardly the Nobel,' Barney scoffed.

'Don't you see, Barney? The whole idea of my *nom de plume* was to remain invisible. Now I'm going to be exposed. What in the name of God am I goin' to do?' Francie was beginning to look desperate.

'Well, if you're asking me …' Barney began.

'Aye, I thought I was,' Francie replied, shaking his head in puzzlement.

'Okay. In that case, I think you've got three options.' Barney paused and rolled the chocolate around in his mouth.

'And what might they be?' Francie raised his head, slowly bracing himself.

'Option one,' Barney said, supping on his cappuccino. 'Be gracious. Thank them most sincerely for the honour, but tell them you have some medical condition. Just say you simply can't make it.'

'Medical condition? Like what?'

'I don't know, leprosy or something?'

'Leprosy!' Francie was getting loud.

A young couple at the next table clearly heard him and they smiled in a condescending way at Barney. An older woman, who was sitting next to the window, moved her chair closer to the door.

'Gee, thanks, Francie. I'll have to wear a bell round my neck on my next visit.'

'I'm sorry. It's just this thing's really getting to me,' Francie said.

'Well, you know what they say: if you live a double life, someday it'll sneak up behind you and bite you on the backside.'

'Thanks a million. I'm running out of road here, and all you can do is make wise-cracks. I need help, fast,' Francie said.

'Well, of course, there's always option two ...'

'What's that when it's at home?'

'Just tell the truth. Stand up like a man. Well, in this case ... you know what I mean.'

Francie shook his head and took in a laboured chestful of air and exhaled.

'Not funny, Barney.'

'I can see you're really worked up about this. It's not like you,' Barney said.

'It doesn't bear thinking about. Jeez, can you imagine wee McMonagle next door? Bloody retired schoolteacher. You know what he's like. Smug little know-it-all. I can just see him sniggering at me over his Escallonia floribunda.'

'Esca— what?'

'Nothing. Then there are all my oul' Post Office mates. My God, I'll never live it down.'

'You're goin' to have to come out of the closet sometime,' Barney said.

'I'm not gay, for God's sake!'

The young couple smiled again. The older woman couldn't move any further away. But Barney could see her buttocks clenching. It was as if she were trying to tuck her bum under the table, the way a dog pulls its tail in when it's frightened.

'Francie, you're gettin' loud again.'

'Sorry. But what am I goin' to do?'

Barney supped generously on his cappuccino and stared aimlessly out onto the Strand Road. He watched a stout woman pass the window and wait at the pedestrian lights on the corner. There was something about her build and fashion style that rang a bell. Then, abruptly, his eyes returned to Francie. Barney had a broad grin on his face.

'Well?' Francie said.

'I have it. I have it now. This is the big one: option three.' Barney looked directly into Francie's eyes. He paused, considering his words carefully before he spoke.

'What? What is it? What's option three?' Francie said.

'Are you sure you're ready for this now? This'll take courage now.'

'Yes! For God's sake, just spit it out.'

'*Tootsie*!' Barney said and opened both his palms for emphasis, like a book. It was as if he'd just revealed the meaning of life.

'What? *Tootsie*! I don't get it,' Francie was clearly confused.

'You know … Dustin Hoffman. When he dressed up as a mature woman in the film *Tootsie*!'

'Ah, no way. I'm not a bloody transvestite. There's no way you're getting me into a frock.' Francie thought he was going to explode.

The young couple looked at each other and giggled. The older woman gathered her things and stood up. Before she left, she gave Barney a look.

'Francie, give me a chance, for heaven's sake. I like this place. I mean, they do a really nice cappuccino. If you don't mind, I'd like to be allowed back.'

'I'm sorry. But I mean – *Tootsie*! Are you mad?'

'Well, I wouldn't dismiss it out of hand, not right away.' Barney considered the shape of Francie's face. 'I mean, give it a chance. You're bald for a start. You've plenty of options when it comes to wigs. If you shave off that goatee and add a little rouge and lipstick, you never know.' Barney gave a mock pout.

'Ah, will you stop.' Francie wasn't having any of it.

'No, seriously. I could talk to Pat Quigley, you know, the local playwright. She could give you a few lessons. I'm sure she has some contacts in the make-up and costume department,' Barney insisted.

'Are you right in the head? No way. It would never work.'

'Might be good to get in touch with your feminine side. Sure after all, isn't that your forte?'

'Very funny,' Francie scowled.

* * *

'I can't believe we're actually here,' Francie said, looking at the throng of women filling the Buncrana Library. 'There's none of them under fifty-five. Dear God, if we're not careful, they'll eat us alive.'

'It's okay for you. I'm in agony here. I hope you're happy,' Barney said.

'It was your flamin' idea,' Francie replied.

'Yes, but why did I have to be Tootsie?'

'Look, we've been over this a thousand times. I picked option two. And with you in option three, we can blend in. You know, like a mature couple.'

'These tights are making me clammy. I can hardly breathe in this gear. To tell you the truth, I'm feeling a wee bit asthmatic.'

'For God's sake, keep your voice down. You sound like a man.'

'Well, between you and me, the last time I looked I was one. My God, someone's coming over; behave yourself, for God's sake.'

Francie and Barney tried to appear relaxed as a rather sophisticated, tall woman approached carrying a tray.

'Would you like a pastry?' she asked in a cultured English accent.

'No, thanks,' Francie answered.

'What about the lady?' she inquired, referring to Barney.

'I don't mind if I do,' Barney enunciated in his best female voice and selected an apple square.

'It's not often we have husbands and wives at our events,' the woman commented.

'Oh, my sister Barbara here, she's a big fan,' Francie said.

'Aren't we all? I'm so looking forward to the presentation,' the woman enthused. She winked coyly at Francie before slipping back into the crowd. The venue was standing room only now. And when she had gone out of earshot, Francie leaned into Barney.

'Barney, I need a drink. Can you see alcohol anywhere?'

'It's a library, not a pub. Anyway, it's Barbara to you, dear.' Barney squeezed Francie's elbow.

'Ah, will you stop. This flamin' tie's choking me. God, I think I'm goin' to faint,' Francie struggled.

'Steady yourself now. Do the breathing exercises Pat Quigley taught you. It'll all be over soon,' Barney said.

Just then, an attractive brunette in her late forties emerged like a fairy godmother. She held a tray of what looked like patterned lemonade glasses.

'Punch, anyone?' she offered in a soft Donegal accent.

'Oh! Cheers,' said Francie, lifting two glasses. He handed one to Barney and knocked his own drink back in a single gulp. Before the tray had moved on, he'd grabbed a second.

'It's all so exciting, isn't it?' the fairy godmother said, looking back over her shoulder.

'You've no idea,' Francie sighed.

'Isn't she somethin'?' Barney whispered.

About twenty minutes later there was a call for order and the tall woman with the English accent had assumed centre stage. She stood beneath a wooden fishing boat that hung suspended from the vaulted ceiling of the converted church. The audience had begun to gather, facing her in a rough semicircle. Francie reckoned if you counted the group sitting in the chairs at the front, there were about sixty people in all. And luckily, both he and Barney had managed to get a seat in the first row. Francie was feeling claustrophobic now and a little lightheaded. There was a makeshift podium with a microphone rigged to it. The woman tapped it with her index finger and it gave an amplified grunt followed by a painful electric squeal. It was temperamental, but it was working.

'Ladies and, of course, gentleman,' she began, nodding at Francie, the only man she could see in the room. There was a gentle wave of laughter and then silence fell again like a blanket. Francie focused on his breathing exercises.

'Firstly, I'd like to introduce myself. My name is Stephanie Temple. As some of you may know, I'm the chair of IWN, the Inishowen Women's Network. I'd like to offer everyone a warm welcome to this, our annual prizegiving night. I'm sure we're all itching to find out who's going to receive the award for best romantic short story, best nature poem and best farmhouse recipe.' Then she drew her arm gracefully above a small table to her left. Standing side by side, there were three glittering trophies mounted on little black plinths. The first was a tiny gold book, the second a small gold inkwell and the third was a little gold rolling pin. They each had a plaque with IWN 2010 inscribed on them.

'Which one's yours, then?' Barney teased.

'I shouldn't have had that punch. I think I might be sick,' Francie whispered, raising a shaking palm to his mouth.

'Breathe deeply, dear,' Barney whispered back in a mocking female tone.

The woman continued. 'We are all, I'm sure, avid readers and fans of Johanna Bamford Smith's writing. It's hard to believe, but it's ten years since her stories first appeared in *Women's Fireside Journal*. And in that time, she has tickled the funny bone of our memories, comforted our aching hearts and touched our very souls,' Stephanie said, touching her heaving bosom.

'God, there's a guy with a camera waiting in the wings. Jeez, it's wee Hughie McLaughlin from the *Journal*,' Francie whispered.

'Where?' Barney said.

'Nine o'clock. On your left.'

'What's that in English?'

'On your left, behind the Mind and Body section. He's hiding behind a big pink-coloured hardback.'

'I see him now. Dear God, I think he's got the lens trained on us. We'll be centrefold in Hughie's Picture Parade in Friday's *Journal*,' Barney said.

Stephanie spoke again. 'As you all know, Johanna Bamford Smith has lived the life of a gifted recluse. And only a few trusted colleagues have been lucky enough to meet her in person. Well, tonight I have a very special treat for everyone, an exclusive for IWN. I've just this very minute received a text from Johanna's agent confirming that she's agreed to make tonight's presentations. And I can confirm that she's actually in the room.'

There was an audible surge of excitement from the audience. And everyone, including Francie and Barney, turned to look behind them.

'God, I don't think I can cope with this,' Francie said.

'Would Johanna Bamford Smith please come up to the podium?' Stephanie announced. And with that, she began to clap, initiating an eager round of applause.

Francie shifted visibly in his seat, torn between staying and running as fast as he could out of the room. But just as Barney squeezed his elbow, somewhere within himself he found a steely inner resolve. He stood up slowly, walked calmly towards Stephanie, stopped at the microphone, turned to face the audience and said, 'I'd like to say a few words, if I may.' He cleared his throat and continued. 'My name is Francie Boyle. I've been a widower for eleven years now. And I live in a wee terraced house in Derry's Garden City.' He took a deep breath and exhaled slowly.

Stephanie placed her left hand discreetly on Francie's lower back in a gesture of gentle support.

'But tonight I have a confession to make, one which I'd like to share with everyone in this room,' he said.

Stephanie moved closer, smiling warmly at him.

'Tonight, it gives me great pleasure, as the writer Johanna Bamford Smith, to present the Two Thousand and Ten Inishowen Women's Network Awards.'

Hughie McLaughlin quickly swung round in front of Francie and Stephanie.

'Bit of a Jekyll and Hyde, aren't we, Francie?' he laughed and pressed the shutter.

INK FINDING PAPER

With all the energy of a child's painting, the sun shimmered in the clear blue of a summer sky. And below the sky, near the village of Muff, reed beds skirted the riverbank. Here and there, they gave way to the low-lying pastures of a small dairy farm. At the farm's south-facing boundary stood Kilderry Wood, a remnant of the ancient oaks that had given it its name. At the edge of the wood was a neat row of recently established back gardens. Newly planted apple trees, shrubs and colourful bedding plants embellished a swathe of fresh grass. Each plot was bordered by low ranch-type fencing that ran from the front driveways along the length of each house and back towards the limit of the wood.

In the third garden, nearest the village, there was a swing. It was bright green, with two red seats. A boy sat on one of the seats, his body twisting gently to the left, then to the right. The toes of his sandals strained to reach the young grass shoots below him. His hands gripped the two lengths of chain suspended from the frame that seemed to tower above him. Lifting his hand to shield his eyes, he squinted. In doing so, his upper lip raised to reveal a gap of missing front teeth. His tongue explored the ridge of gum that had formed and for a moment, he imagined the day his new teeth would arrive.

Soon, he would be going to school at the top of the hill. St Brigid's National School was just a two-minute walk from his front door. And from where he was sitting, he could see the top of the chain-link fence bordering the playground. Rising above the fence was a metal pole, fixed to a square white board above a red basketball net. A smile of anticipation lit up his face. Then his gaze drifted back over the roof of his house and travelled down to his neighbour's bedroom window. Perhaps his best friend Lisa might be looking out. Then she would see him and wave as she always did and come out to play.

'Lisa lazybones,' he called.

Catherine, the boy's mother, was at the kitchen sink. She could hear him calling to Lisa and she sensed he was restless. When she had placed the last of their breakfast plates on the metal drainer, she opened the window and shouted out to him.

'Matthew! I have a surprise for you. Come and get it!'

Matthew leapt from the red seat, sending it jiggling, and ran to the kitchen. His mother wiped her hands on her jeans and picked up a small plastic bottle with a yellow lid. She unscrewed it quickly, and when his silhouette entered the bright rectangle of the open door, she blew bubbles up and over his blond hair and out into the garden. He blinked and, like a kitten, he pawed at the delicate, glistening spheres trembling and quivering above him. Then he giggled and ran out to catch them. When all the bubbles had burst between his fingers or escaped to float high into the air, she handed him the bottle with its blowing-stick. With her left hand, she cupped the back of his head, her fingers playing with the locks of his hair. A memory formed vividly in her mind of Matthew sitting on a chair in the kitchen, his eyelashes trembling beneath the scissors in her hand. She is trimming his fringe for the first time.

Catherine smiled now as Matthew excitedly withdrew the stick from the soapy liquid and blew forcefully. Soon, he was running in crude circles around the garden, his right arm outstretched, trailing streams of tiny bubbles as if marking the boundaries of his world.

'Look at me, Lisa lazybones,' he called, now and then glancing up to Lisa's bedroom window. But no-one came. When all the bubbles were gone, he dropped the bottle with its yellow blowing-stick among a cluster of buttercups. He heard a telephone ring and turned to watch his mother re-enter the house. When she disappeared into the shadows of the hallway, his attention wandered until it was drawn to the dancing flight of a white butterfly. Eagerly, he tracked its journey around the swing. And, just as his mother had taught him, he placed his two thumbs together, palms facing away from him, and flapped the fingers of both hands.

'Flutter bye, butterfly, flutter bye,' he sang as he continued to trace its erratic journey. It dipped and rose and rested, then rose again and drifted until it had travelled to the edges of his garden along the threshold of the woods. Perhaps it wanted him to follow, he thought. Intrigued, he did so. Cautiously, he stepped onto the lower rung of the back fence. He wobbled as his hands clasped the second upper length of wood. Carefully, he straddled it and persisted until he had lifted both his legs over to the other side. Then he dropped silently onto the ground below.

'Where are you, butterfly?' he said and turned to face the coolness of the woods. His eyes scanned the looming shade until once again the delicate flickering wings beckoned, a milky light among the trees.

'I can see you. Here I come,' he said and his skin registered a change as tiny goose bumps spread slowly up his arms, across his pale shoulders and over the back of his neck. Unconcerned, he trampled gently into the wood until the soft clover beneath his sandals had become the dry snap of twigs.

* * *

'I love and approve of myself,' Catherine repeated for the third time. And the twist of flame from the open fire seemed to murmur in response. On the slate roof, pitched just above her, snow fell, its flakes wide and silent. Light entered the room from a small east-facing window. The wooden frame still housed its original sash, the pulley-rope rigid with discoloured paint. All four panes were misted with condensation and the glass in the bottom right was cracked. The makeshift repair of brittle sticky-tape was the colour of nicotine. On the sill, tangled among wisps of cobweb, was a crusted bluebottle carcass. A small table stood next to the window, its plastic tablecloth faded, the pattern barely illuminated by the weak winter light.

Wearing a heavy black woollen, Catherine sat at the table, her attention drifting away from the window and back towards the shadows in the room. And the gloom seemed to beckon her as if wanting to invite this broken version of herself into its dark embrace. Increasingly, Catherine felt she was dissolving into the world around her. Reality had become more like the conté sketches her husband Paul had shown her years before when they were dating. Paul, an art teacher, had loved Georges Seurat's studies in tone. He explained how the extremities of one thing had been rendered to bleed into the boundaries of the other. Now, looking at her coat hanging from the hook on the door, it appeared to seep into the armchair sitting in front of it. And the armchair, the more she stared at it, too, was merging with the bookshelf beside it. Even her books, she fancied, were blending into one. Her flesh, her thoughts, her things, all seemed to blot, like ink finding paper.

Her memories were all that sustained her now. Daily, she struggled to replay the sound of Matthew's voice. Her greatest fear being that its music would fade until it became but a receding echo in her head. In recent months, writing – placing her thoughts where she could see them – had become a ritual. Exhaling heavily, she closed her eyes and rested her face in her raised, open palms. Moments later, she lifted her head to watch the snowflakes accumulate diagonally on the glass. Out on the road, a steady stream of cars and 4X4s negotiated the weather. In the middle distance stood a bank of fuchsia, winter thin. Above the fuchsia, a scatter of crows blew across the snow-laden sky and drifted out towards the edges of the river.

'I live in the now; each moment is new,' she said, this time louder than before. She pushed back on her chair, its legs trumpeting against the flagstone floor. Then she reached into the bag at her feet. Her fingers traced the cold metal door key, read the plastic-wrapped tissues and the engraved detail of a metal hip flask. Briefly, she tested its weight. It was empty, had been for almost a year now. But still she carried it. A reminder. Then finding her black notebook and fountain pen, she brought them up to the table; opening her book, she turned to a fresh page and started to write. Always, it began loosely, words falling onto the page, unconcerned with sense, slowly accumulating. Often, they came in twos and threes. She wrote them as they arrived:

Leaves, scattered flake-like,
On a cold white crust,
Make the landscape taste of ochre,
On the tongue of winter.

Catherine paused, then rotated the fountain pen between her fingers until she could see the engraved inscription on the side: 'Happy Christmas, Mum, 2007. Love, Matthew & Dad', it read. Almost two years had passed since Matthew's death. Yet her guilt remained fresh as ever. In those first days, it was all-consuming. Dr Halcomb, her GP, had recommended something to soften the initial blow; he had prescribed Zitolipram. But then, once or twice, she found that if she washed it down with a glass of wine, she could blur the edges for just that little longer. Soon, she was drinking during the day ... then it was every day. And Catherine discovered she could postpone the need to unpack her dark and twisted thoughts.

'You're going to drown yourself, too – in drink!' Paul had said.

'What do you mean, drown myself, *too*?'

'You're drinking every day; you're mixing medication with alcohol!'

'Don't pretend you don't understand what you said. You're blaming me for Matthew's death! That's what you meant. That's what you really think. Isn't it, Paul?'

'I never said that!'

'You don't need to. You can't even give a straight answer, can you? It's the truth. It's what everyone thinks, everyone in this bloody street. "Catherine allowed her little boy to wander off into the woods, and while she was chatting on the phone, he drowned in the fucking river." Isn't that what everyone's saying?'

'Catherine, that's not what I meant.'

'Don't lie to me. Even your own mother, she almost said as much to me this morning!'

And so it went on. Every time they spoke to each other, they argued, until their relationship was nothing but a fall of dead leaves at their feet. If they talked now, it was only to finalise the finances from the sale of their house in Muff.

Meeting Helen, her counsellor, over a year ago had been a turning point. Helen supported her, eased Catherine into recovery.

'I'm here to help you face your abandoned feelings,' Helen soothed.

And as the months passed, somehow Catherine found the strength to relive the scene: when they brought her to him, his body, pinned among the reeds, limp and sodden from the brackish river water. The shock of his cold head in her cupped palm had unhinged her, sucked the strength from her legs and dragged her screaming to her knees.

'Seeing my Matthew inside the tiny box, and later it sinking into the gaping dark …' She shook her head. 'The pure white against the muck and the earth.' Then she broke down and wept. And through snatches of breath she said, 'It turned all my answers to questions, Helen.'

But living in the old cottage that was now her home, Catherine found it strangely comforting. All the impressions left behind seemed to reassure her. Whole days had drifted by where she simply stared at the blank frames of dust on the walls, her mind trying to imagine the pictures that once hung there. Her few small rooms invited thoughts of the old man who had shuffled through them. The armchair still held his shape. It was as though she were not alone. And when the estate agent had told her old blind Conal used to keep a canary for company, she had replied, 'How tender, Matthew would really have loved that,' and had signed the year's lease. Increasingly, she felt a connection with the old man, with a life spent negotiating through a world of shadows. As time passed, she began to sense a memory of his touch on the peeling wallpaper.

It was Helen who had encouraged her to write, to see it as a way of talking to Matthew. Since then, she hadn't stopped. Her thoughts gathered again and she began to place them on the page:

All around my outer self,
This liquid of land and sky,
Now bleeds to indigo.

Later that afternoon, Catherine was standing on the coastal path between Moville and Greencastle. For some time, she had been staring vacantly across the river at the high-sculpted face of Binevenagh on the opposite shore. Then, quite suddenly, as if waking from a spell, she walked down to the edge of the shoreline. She removed a small container from her pocket, leaned forward and placed it in the sand in front of her. And for a moment, she let her thoughts return to that morning when she lifted it from among the buttercups in their back garden.

'How can the sun still shine?' she had cried and stared as a bumblebee had lumbered over the bright yellow petals.

Now, standing with the toes of her boots at the water's edge, she opened her notebook and leafed to her writing earlier in the day. The sound of a page being torn was barely audible under the bickering of seagulls above. She folded the writing as though wrapping a child in a blanket. Then she slipped the paper into the bottle, sealing tight its bright yellow lid. The tide was flowing fast, out towards the mouth of the lough, well beyond the shores that she knew. She cast the bottle into the water and watched it sink briefly, then re-emerge to bob and flow with the current.

Catherine turned, stepping between the boulders and the seaweed strewn before her. And without looking back, she moved silently through falling snow.

Some Other Country

It all started one night in Sandino's bar, about a year ago. You know, the pub that backs onto the bus station, at the end of Water Street. Thursdays and Fridays are good craic. But this was a Tuesday and I wasn't expecting anything special.

Standing at the bar, I'd taken a few sups from my pint. I was daydreaming. It was April and the days were stretching. The usual suspects were there. A few stools away, Billy and Locky were arguing over God knows what. Aoife and Twy were smooching behind me in their regular spot near the door. I couldn't see them, but I could hear the girls giggling. I was staring aimlessly past the spirit bottles. Reflected in the bar mirror, I saw Seamy, Heather and the others outside acting the goat. They were laughing. You know the craic, taking a smoke break. I'd given up fags a while back. So I was minding their drinks, just happy to be on my own for a bit.

'So, what's your story?' I heard someone say from over my left shoulder.

The voice was female, foreign and, I guessed, French. I didn't respond at first, didn't want to make a dick of myself. I was pretty sure she was talking to someone else. So I downed another mouthful of Guinness.

'Not a Derryman, then?' she said.

Then I realised it *was* me she was chatting to. So I turned and smiled. 'You bet I am. And from the Bog, you know, the Bogside. No better man you'll ever meet.'

When I shook her hand, the cold of her palm and fingers surprised me. But she was lovely. Taking in her dark eyes, I caught a glimpse of platted black hair running down past her neck. She had that hint of fine fluff below her earlobes and jaw line, dark and delicate. One of those loose-fitting scarves circled her throat. To be honest, I was flattered.

'Decky,' I said, offering my hand. I was about to buy her a drink when I spotted she had a glass of Guinness.

'Véronique. Your hands are beautiful,' she responded, releasing my grip.

I gave a mock frown, inviting her to tell me more.

'Cosy,' she said. 'You Irish are so warm-blooded.'

'Aren't we all?'

'Believe me, for a woman from Dinan, it's freezing.'

'Dinan? That would be Brittany, right?'

'Very good.' She flashed her eyebrows, clearly impressed.

Of course, I was chancing my arm. I had a vague memory: Davy, this mate of mine who's really into Irish music, had gigged at a festival there a few years back. But sometimes I find a pint can give you wee insights, too.

'Can I borrow your hands?' she asked.

'Now there's an invitation. I'm your man.'

She pointed both hands at me like a child praying and nodded for me to cup and rub them between my palms. Christ, I couldn't believe it. I just did it. We laughed out loud like we'd known each other for ages. It was only when Seamy and Heather came back in that I snapped out of it.

'Well, looky here, if it's not Declan Magee playing Patty Cake,' Seamy said.

I did the introductions. But after a while, I managed to ease them out of our space. I just wanted to chat freely. Didn't want it all played back to me the next day. As the night went on, I gathered that she was running some kind of language classes in the Central Library. She said it was only a small group but that they were a nice mix of different ages.

'You're not going to believe this, but I've never been in there,' I told her, nodding towards the library.

'Why not?'

And I could tell she was genuinely shocked. After all, it was literally across the road from the pub. Well, you know how it is. After a few, you tend to spill your personal stuff. Let's face it. We all do it.

'You remember earlier when you asked me what my story was?' I continued.

'I do.'

'Hey, not so fast. I haven't asked you to marry me yet.'

She burst into a laugh. You know, like a child, so full of fun. She let it out like it was a bird, up into the air. I'd had a few pints at this stage and I was starting to lose the grip of myself. You know, I was in a groove with her. Now and then I caught a glimpse of Seamy and he was pouting his lips and blowing me big fat kisses. I did my best to keep a straight face. But I was buzzin'.

'Well,' she made a mock frown, 'are you going to keep me waiting?'

I took a final gulp of my pint and looked straight into her eyes. 'Véronique, I can't read or write. Not properly anyway.' I just told her.

'Decky!' Her face lit up in surprise. She put her hand on my arm.

'Listen, I'm not joking!'

'No, I believe you. It's just that's what I do. I teach literacy. Please, you must come to the library. There are only six people and they're really friendly,' she said.

'I thought you were teaching French or Breton?'

'No, it's English. You really must come,' she said. And she gave me a look like I was a wounded bird and she specialised in broken wings.

'I don't know. I feel really daft now. I mean, here you are, teaching Irish people how to read and write English and you're a French speaker from Brittany. I feel like an eejit.'

'Tell you what,' she said. 'Come to my class next week and we have a date.'

Well, there was no contest. Was there?

'What do I have to do?' I said.

'It's all very gentle reading exercises. And next week, I have a poet coming in. He's reading some of his work at the end of class.'

'Who?'

'Tom DeButleir.'

'Ah, Jesus,' I said. I didn't know him, but I'd seen him strolling around the town like a bloody Irish chieftain. You know the type, all forehead and long hair, with deep, meaningful thoughts. He was about my age. Handsome, too. And he knew it.

'He thinks he's special, I know,' she said. 'But he's not my type. Honest. I'll need you there, Decky, to keep him in his place.' She winked at me.

The way she pronounced my name, 'Deckee', it was pure magic.

'I'll be there,' I said.

Véronique's class wasn't too bad. She surprised me. Made me realise how much I already knew. It was all women, too, so no complaints there. Véronique, she's good, though. She has an easy way with her. I'd never had that with a teacher before. So I agreed to take it one week at a time. Later, during the tea break, we all chatted for a bit and then arranged our chairs in a semicircle. Véronique, she gave a brief introduction to yer man, the poet.

Christ, though, Tom DeButleir, what a jerk! He swannies in like some Hollywood actor. You know the score: all physical presence with a hint of wild angst. Of course, the women in the class, they instantly warm to him. You can almost feel it as you sit there. Anyway, he reads one boring bloody poem after the other and he lingers on certain words like he's savouring expensive ice cream. I hated that. Especially when he finished one particular piece with a really naff description. I think it was something like A Mackerel Sky. All the women just lapped it up. It sounded like they were eating the same bloody ice cream. 'Mmm,' they said. Now that drove me mad. I wanted to jump up and say to them all, 'Look, this guy's a bloody wanker. Can't you tell, for Christ's sake?' But I didn't; instead, I just sank lower in my seat. I knew if he caught my eye he'd be thinking, *you're the real sucker for turning up*. And the worst part was I agreed with him.

'Listen, I don't care if he *is* a poet, he's a bloody poser,' I whispered to Véronique afterwards in Sandino's. Of course, DeButleir had made his way over to the pub, too. But, thank God, the class fan club had sidetracked him.

'Véronique, you could be reading the bloody grocery list and I'd listen to you all day. But you see Casanova ...' I said, nodding at DeButleir.

'I know,' she said. 'And I think the sound of your voice is beautiful, too.'

The way she said 'beautifool'. Ah!

So I kept going to Véronique's classes and we kept meeting. Sometimes it was for coffee or a pint. A few times we went to hear bands in the Gweedore or the Bound for. Véronique also invited women writers to read at the class, you know, novelists, short-story writers and songwriters. After a while, I really enjoyed listening and thinking about what they wrote. Véronique, she helped us realise that writing isn't really stuffy at all. It's a way of expressing yourself. You know, so that people could get a handle on where you were coming from.

After a few months, Véronique and I started going out as a couple. I read every day. All of a sudden, it was as if my world got bigger. I began to read all sorts of stuff, anything, junk mail and food labels. For God's sake, she even caught me at the dentist's the other day reading *Ireland's*-bloody-*Own*. She told me about the movies of François Truffaut and ideas like New-Wave cinema. And here was me thinking those black-and-white French films were just about naked nymphets looking all lost and confused. Then she talked about French Literature, existentialism and yer man Samuel Beckett. Until we both got together, there was so much I hadn't known.

And all I could tell her was what it was like to fail the Eleven-Plus. How, as a kid, I was bored at school so I bunked out of class at lunchtime and headed into Derry and stole packets of Penguin biscuits out of Wellworth's for my lunch. I told her I used to nick CDs from the stalls down by the Guildhall until one day this guy chased me up onto the Walls. He bounded

67

after me like a bloody gazelle. When he caught me, he gave me a slap around the head and took the CD back. Just then, my uncle Aloysius had come strolling past with his nose in the *Journal*. I was sure he must have seen me 'cause I watched him sidestep a dog turd.

'Last night, dodgy penalty, hey,' was all he said. He didn't even look at me.

'Yes, Uncle Al.'

'It was all over for the Candy Stripes in the second half,' he said, then he just walked on, reading his paper. I heard him whistling as he headed down the steps. Véronique told me to put it all down on paper. She said I was a natural storyteller. I just laughed.

'Who'd listen to me? Sure, half of Derry write stories in their heads,' I said. But while she was discovering me, I've been getting to know her, too. Everything about her: it's like I'm seeing it for the first time; the way she stands, her hair, even the wee sounds she makes when we're close. And when we're together – you know, having sex – I love to just lie there and look into her eyes, just as she goes into the pleasure zone. It's magic, like some other country. It all seems so exotic, but at the same time, it's normal.

Anyway, I took Véronique's advice and started to write a bit. Just wee notes to her at the start. Listen, don't laugh. For me this was a big thing. I'd never done it before. And she loves them. I'm not sure if it's because I can write now or if it's what I'm saying in them. But she just laps them up. She's like a wee puppy dog – you know, all tender and playful. The other morning, we are lying there, in bed together. She has this place in an apartment block at the back of KFC and her windows face out over the Foyle. I'm looking at her, and as she's waking up, I'm thinking, *this is the life*. I turn to look out the window. She has this weird thing about keeping them open at night after the lights go out. Anyway, it's a bright morning and I can hear birdsong. A dog somewhere down on the promenade below starts barking, sort of half-hearted, like. Then a pigeon flaps up and lands on the windowsill. After a few seconds, it lumbers off into the air. So I glance up at the sky and it looks different. All the clouds are mottled and spread out at a funny angle. And the sun is radiating all these warm colours up behind them.

'Véronique, you're not going to believe this,' I say.

'What is it?' She's rubbing her eyes and yawning.

'Listen, it's nothing bad,' I say, touching her forehead to reassure her.

'Well, don't keep me waiting,' she says, snuggling up against me. 'What is it?'

'Now, don't laugh. I'm no expert on fish. And for God's sake don't mention this to Tom De-bloody-Butleir.'

'What is it, Decky?' she says – you know, like 'Deckee'.

'I think I can see a mackerel sky.'

'Ah, come on now, Decky. You can do better than that,' she says.

Suddenly, she clasps both my hands and pulls me out of bed. Then she steers me towards the window. And we're both standing there – you know, buck naked – looking up at the morning sun.

'It's beautiful,' she says.

'Like some other country,' I say.

THE RIVER

Hilary had prepared the front reception. She made it welcoming and cosy. But still, she kept it professional looking. After all, this was how she earned a living. She had a new client and they would need privacy. A black marble fireplace with art nouveau tiles surrounded an open cast-iron grate. To the left of a brass carriage clock on the mantelpiece stood a framed photograph of her father. However, the focal point in the room was a teak coffee table. A designer vase held a simple display of lilies, sculptural and scented. Beside the vase sat a porcelain container, its surface decoration masking a vertical stack of tissues at its heart.

Hilary stood at the window and peeked between the Venetian blinds. They were made from light sandalwood, a look she liked. Her attention was drawn to a small white van as it travelled down the hill. It moved slowly, stopping occasionally, the driver checking the house numbers on the opposite side. The van followed the curve of the cul-de-sac until it stopped at the entrance to Hilary's driveway. She remained watching, lifting her heels, free of the tight grip of her shoes, until she glimpsed the driver. A short, solidly built man with thick white hair emerged into the late afternoon sun. He appeared self-conscious but kind, she thought. She noticed he had a limp. And there was something else, a quality she could not quite articulate that unsettled her. She dismissed the feeling and eased her feet back into her shoes. As she turned, her gaze travelled across the picture of her father on the shelf. She smiled and left the room.

Passing the mirror in the hallway, she quickly checked her face and her hair. Then she retreated to the kitchen, where the kettle was on the boil. When she reached the kettle, she placed two cups and a plate of biscuits on a tray. Finally, she waited for the doorbell to ring.

As he turned to face the house and walk up the drive, he was acutely aware of the dirt on his van. The garden was neatly manicured. Protestant looking, he thought, but what did he expect? He was in the genteel environs of the Waterside, on the east bank of the Foyle. A black BMW 4X4 stood gleaming on the tarmac. The front rooms of the surrounding houses appeared empty. Still, he sensed he was being watched. He passed the shrubs edging the corner of the lawn and entered the porch. He cleared his throat and pressed the doorbell. The bell was loud and clear. He watched as the presence of an approaching figure grew on the patterned glass. The door opened and a woman stood in front of him. She reached forward and shook his hand.

'You must be Finbar. I'm Hilary. Please come in.' She took a step back and gestured towards a door on the left, just off the hallway.

'Would you like tea or coffee?' she asked.

'A mug of tea, if you don't mind, please,' Finbar said. Maria, his wife, was right, he thought. 'Once you're through the front door, you'll be fine,' she'd told him. 'It's all about being yourself, Finbar, dear. Your feelings *do* matter. Tell her what's worrying you,' she had said.

When Finbar entered the room, he was immediately impressed by its bright, relaxed colour scheme. It had that airy feel; neat, with everything in its place. Probably rarely used, he suspected. The sofa was big, generous and leather. In the corner, near the open fireplace, stood a wooden armchair. Its simple firmness appealed to him. He walked towards it and sat down.

Hilary returned carrying a tray. It held two mugs of tea, a small jug of milk and a plate of large oatmeal cookies. As she set the tray on the table, Finbar noticed her figure. Early forties at most, he guessed. Striking was the word he would use later when Maria asked him. Hilary was almost young enough to be his daughter; and for a moment he wanted to leave, had a powerful urge to say that he'd changed his mind, that he was sorry for wasting her time and that it was all a mistake.

'Milk, sugar?'

'Just a splash of milk, thanks.'

'Cookie?'

'No, thanks. I recently joined Weight Watchers,' he said and blushed.

'Really? Good for you. Core or Points programme?'

'I'm counting the Points.'

'Fantastic! How's it going?'

'I've lost nine pounds in five weeks,' he said.

'Well done!' she said, clearly impressed. 'So you've got your first Silver Seven?'

'Aye!' He allowed an embarrassed smile to soften his face.

Hilary took a seat at the end of the sofa, nearest the hearth. She faced the window, looked directly at Finbar and sipped her tea.

As the light fell on her hair, suddenly he felt the intimacy of the moment and he tensed.

'Forty pounds, wasn't it? Do I pay you now or at the end?' he said, slipping his right hand into his jacket pocket. This was strange, he thought, being vulnerable with a woman he didn't know and handing her money. It felt embarrassing.

'Please, it's fine. We can discuss payment later. Let's just settle for a minute or two, enjoy our tea.'

After a few moments of silence, Hilary spoke again.

'I'd like you to know I'm here to listen. I'm not here to judge you. It's important you understand that, Finbar. Is it okay to call you Finbar?'

'Finbar is fine.'

'Good. Please call me Hilary. Well, I want you to feel that you can trust me. Try to see me as someone who can support you. I'm here to help as best I can. From what you told me on the phone, you've experienced a hugely traumatic event. But before we talk about that, I'd like to get to know Finbar a little better. So in your own time, there's no hurry, just tell me about yourself, your family, anything you feel comfortable to share.'

Finbar took a gulp of tea followed by a deep breath. He avoided looking at Hilary; instead, he stared at the orange petals of the lilies in front of him.

He cleared his throat. 'To be honest, Hilary, I almost didn't come. I mean, I'm a sixty-two-year-old man, for God's sake. It seems silly to be sitting here talking to you about myself, about my feelings.' Then he did look at Hilary, waiting for her to comment. But she remained silent and returned his gaze patiently.

He began again. 'I'm a house painter, nothing special, have been since my teens. Married, with two boys. Eleanor, my only daughter, she died twenty years ago. She had CF, you know, cystic fibrosis. We did all we could. She was a real fighter, but with her lungs, she was hardly ever out of Altnagelvin Hospital. She'd pick up an infection from a sneeze. To listen to her cough, it was terrible. And then, when she was thirteen, we lost her.'

Finbar clicked his middle finger and thumb.

'Just like that, life can be taken from you. Especially in this bloody place. Anyway, she was gone. It was a terrible blow for Maria at the time. Maria, she's my wife. She was the one who recommended this "psychology thing".' He loosely gestured towards Hilary and the room.

'I'm sorry to hear about your daughter. How did you cope?' Hilary shifted slightly and leaned forward.

'Myself, I just kept working. But the circumstances of her death, that's a whole other story. Eleanor, being our only girl, the two boys took it bad, although things have levelled out a bit now that the lads are grown. Martin, my eldest, he runs Cavanagh Construction. He's building that new development in Inishowen. River View, it's called. You've probably seen the ads in the *Journal*. Anyway, I work for him. Me and my other son, Owen, he's a joiner.' He took another gulp of tea.

'It's hard losing close family members. I know,' Hilary said.

'Sorry, I didn't realise.'

'Not to worry, Finbar.' She paused. 'Now, I know we've talked briefly on the phone. But lately, what has been happening?'

'I can't seem to get the incident last month out of my head. I rarely cross the doorstep now. I haven't taken wee Emma-Louise for an ice cream in weeks. Emma-Louise, she's my granddaughter. Christ, I have these night sweats. I have this recurring nightmare. It's as if something is waiting for me, lurking in the shadows. Mostly, I find I can't breathe when it comes over me.'

* * *

A week later, Hilary had an A4 file pad resting across her knees and she was reading from her notes. Finbar was sitting on his usual chair, clasping his mug of tea between his hands, enjoying its warmth.

'Well, how have things been with you this last while?' she inquired.

'To be honest, I think they're getting worse.'

'I see.' She tapped her pen on her pad. 'Finbar, I thought this week we could talk in more detail about your last day at work. Do you feel up to doing that?'

An image of the Lifford greyhound track formed itself in Finbar's mind. Suddenly, he felt as though a starting gate had flung open in front of him and away he went.

'Okay. Well, I can't imagine how I could ever go back to the site, not now. I can't seem to get the image out of my head. If it weren't so tragic ... I mean. I spent the morning loading up the van. You know, the usual: the ladders, the rollers and the paint; my favourite emulsion brush; I remember fanning the bristles to check they were clean. Then I stuck it into my dungarees. Jesus! I was whistling *Only Our Rivers Run Free*, for God's sake. My lunch box, you know, the usual, an old McVitie's tin, it was sitting there. I take an apple, one of my five-a-day, along with my corned-beef sandwiches. Anyway, the lid wasn't closed right. It was resting on top of some bits of sandpaper. I could see the piece of cake. Maria, she'd baked it on the Sunday, you see. And I can clearly remember I was looking forward to scoffing down the fruitcake. I had packed a big fat slice. I was smiling away to myself, picturing it in my hand, and me supping on my mug during the tea break. Jesus! When I think about it now, I could cry.'

Finbar raised his hand to his mouth for a moment.

'Take your time,' Hilary said.

After a moment, he gathered himself and spoke again. 'So much for my wee routine. It all seems so trivial now by comparison. I mean, there I was, setting up for a day's work. I'd even brought along my CD player. Wee Emma-Louise, she gave me a CD of some classical music and I was all set to blast it around the house, once all the lads got started. It was something about the seasons, aye, *Four Seasons*, that's it. Anyway, I knew the lads would slag me off, but to be honest, I like the slagging. The day just slides by when you get a bit of banter going.

'At first, when I arrived, I thought Owen must have opened up the house early for us. I knew everyone was under pressure. The whole scheme was running late and some of the couples were worried about losing their deposits. They were caught in a chain, what with the slump and their own houses not shifting. I'd heard a number of them were back on the market. Some of the couples had lost their jobs. Anyway, I'd gone upstairs to open a few windows. Dan had started brushing the floors and there was bloody dust everywhere. It really gets me in the chest. I'd fucking told him. Damp it down, I said. But was he listening? At eight-thirty in the morning? Nah, of course he wasn't.'

Finbar took another gulp of tea.

'There's no rush now,' Hilary said.

'It was the draught from the open hatch into the roof space that made me look up. Christ! I knew immediately as soon as I saw the black shoes. You know the ones, stylish but flat, plain looking, like school shoes. They were hanging just below the level of the hatch. She was swaying slightly, almost the way you'd see a child dangling their legs on a swing, if you know

78

what I mean. I tried to call out to the lads, but what with the dust and my bloody chest, nothing came out. I just can't get it out of my head. Christ! She was only twenty-four. She'd it all to fucking play for. Fuck, what a waste.'

* * *

Now at his third session, Finbar was still sceptical about the whole thing. Hilary kept going on about the work he was doing on his feelings. What work? This wasn't work. It was just chitchat. If they'd been two women, he'd have said they were gossiping. If anything, Finbar was sure this 'therapy' thing was going nowhere. The nightmares were getting worse. And now he was having what Hilary called 'anxiety attacks'.

'Finbar, do you mind if we backtrack a bit? You mentioned your daughter in the first session.'

'Eleanor? Yes, what about her?'

'Well, I just wondered if we could talk a little about her. Would you mind?' Hilary flipped through the pages of her notepad until she found what she was looking for. 'I think you said that your wife, Maria, and the two boys, Martin and Owen, had taken Eleanor's death badly and that you had just got on with things, that you had focused on your work. Is that a fair way to describe what happened?' She looked at him and let the pages fall back into place on her notepad.

'Aye, I suppose that's fair.'

'Could you talk a little about the circumstances of Eleanor's death? Do you think you could go back to the day she died?'

Finbar took in a chestful of air.

'Well, it started off as a normal day for us. Eleanor had been poorly the previous few weeks. But with CF, it was routine for her. She was always very brave. Stoic, aye, I think that's the word Maria always used. But when the accumulation in Eleanor's lungs got too much, she needed to be hospitalised. We had to wait until there was an ICU bed available for her, you know, intensive care. Almost like a private room, you might say. She was so prone to infections.'

'So you got her into a bed in Altnagelvin, then?'

'No. That's just it. We didn't make it across the river. Twenty-odd years ago, Derry, the North, it was a very different place. You're probably too young to remember, Hilary.'

'I remember the time very well, Finbar. But please, continue.'

'An undercover soldier had been killed. And the Brits went on the rampage. Of course, we all know it wasn't their first time, especially in this town. Anyway, they'd blocked off the Craigavon and Foyle bridges. You know, to keep the west bank, to keep us natives, in our place.'

'Is that how you would have seen it?'

'Hilary, it was standard operating procedure!'

'Sorry, Finbar. Please continue.'

'Well, I didn't realise until I'd turned onto the Foyle Bridge that it was closed. I was caught in a tailback. They'd reduced the lanes to one and I couldn't turn the bloody van around. Eleanor, she was lying in her school uniform on a mattress in the back of the van. Her head was propped up on a few pillows. I could hear her wheezing terribly. And I was trying not to let her know there was a hold-up. I kept saying, don't worry, darling, we're nearly there. But I could see that the Brits were tense. Then one of them up on the crest of the bridge started firing live rounds into the line of traffic. We were like sittin' bloody ducks. It was mayhem.'

'How dreadful.' Hilary shook her head slightly. 'I'm genuinely shocked. To think the security forces would do such a thing!'

'Hilary, you're not serious? Take it from me. It was payback time. You know, for the undercover guy. The next thing I know, a bullet punches through my windscreen. I couldn't see a thing. The glass was suddenly like a mosaic pattern, a mass of tiny cracks. And there was a hole as big as a grapefruit where the round had entered. I heard it whizzing out through the back. My first thought was for Eleanor. My legs were like jelly. I jumped out, ran around the side and opened the back doors. I could tell by the way the soles of her school shoes were resting on the mattress, I knew she was dead.

The shock, it had just been too much for her wee heart, Hilary. There wasn't a mark on her. She wasn't hit. But it was only when I tried to lift her that I realised that the bullet had gone straight through my thigh. I collapsed down onto the road.'

Hilary passed the porcelain container to Finbar. He withdrew a clump of tissues and began to cry.

* * *

Another week had passed. Finbar sat listening to the sound of tea being poured in the kitchen. He glanced at the photograph on the mantelshelf and picked it up. It was of a man in his late forties. He was dressed in khaki, waxed fishing gear and appeared to be standing in the rain. A brightly coloured fishing fly adorned the lapel of his jacket. His bright face beamed out at Finbar.

'Murray T Hetherington,' Hilary said as she entered the room and placed the tray on the table. 'Daddy, to be precise.'

Somehow the name seemed familiar to Finbar and for a moment he was thrown. 'Of course, Hetherington, that's your maiden name,' he said, composing himself. 'So he's a man who enjoys a spot of fishing, then?'

'Used to. Sadly, Daddy's dead.'

'I'm sorry, I didn't mean to …'

'He was a boat builder,' she said, lifting her mood. 'In fact, he made this very table and the chair you're sitting on.' She handed Finbar his tea.

Finbar took the mug and placed his free hand on the wood of his chair. He began caressing the joints where the legs met the frame of the seat, exploring the detailing of the finish with his fingers.

'Beautiful workmanship,' he said.

'Yes. "Never hurry a Murray," he always joked. You know – like the old TV ad for Murray Mints? He loved taking his time, using his hands, working with wood, getting to know its character and shaping it. Really, it was his vocation, that and the great outdoors. And as you can see, he adored fishing.' She took the photograph from Finbar.

'He must have been an interesting father.'

'Yes, he was. My childhood was filled with the smell of sawdust from his overalls. What with his workshop, I used to imagine that I was Laura Ingalls and Daddy was Charles. I'm not sure if you remember the TV series *Little House on the Prairie*,' she said, smiling at the image of her father.

'That's going back a bit. Aye, that was yer man. He also acted in *Bonanza*. Little Joe, wasn't it?'

'That's him.' Hilary smiled widely.

'It must have been a fine workshop.'

'It was. I used to brush all the shavings from the floor in my little dustpan. I remember the smell of pine, teak and cedar. I loved the sound of his plane as it glided along a length of wood. He always whistled while he worked. And sometimes when he stooped and inspected the line of shaved wood, he'd catch my eye and wink at me.'

They sat in silence for a while, supping their tea. Then Hilary turned to Finbar. 'Now, let's talk about Finbar, shall we?'

'Aye, I suppose.'

'Tell me, this recurring nightmare. Is it still a feature?'

'To be honest, it's as bad as ever.'

'Would you mind talking me through it as best you can?'

'It's really strange. I can never remember the beginning, only how it ends. In the dream, I'm at home, upstairs, and I have an awful sense that someone – no, it's more like some-*thing* – is prowling the floor below. It's as if I know it's searching for me and I'm terrified. Anyway, it doesn't make sense, but I walk downstairs to the living room. And when I open the door, it's there. It's hard to describe. It's like a black, brooding presence. I swear to God, every bone in my body is dragging me in the other direction. But I turn towards it, howling like a tormented animal. It's not that I'm screaming, more like I'm howling, and the sound of my howling wakes me. I'm always feverish. Maria, she just holds me until I've calmed myself again.'

Hilary remained silent for a moment while she took some notes. 'Can you remember when you started having this nightmare?' she asked.

'It began not long after Eleanor died. I had it for a number of years. Then it stopped. And now it's back, with a vengeance. It started again just after I found the young woman hanging in the loft.'

'Finbar, in the nightmare, what do you think it is that's waiting for you in your living room?' She glanced up from her notes.

'I don't know. I've never thought about it in that way.'

'It's interesting that in the nightmare you try to enter the room. Despite being terrified, you attempt to face your fear.'

Finbar raised his eyebrows in casual acknowledgement.

'Has the dream ever proceeded beyond that point?'

'Hold on, are you saying my bloody nightmare means something?'

'Have you ever considered that it might?'

'No. Never,' he said.

* * *

One month later, Finbar stood in Hilary's front porch. It was a bitter night and the collar of his jacket was raised against the rain. He pressed the doorbell and waited. As soon as Hilary opened the door, he spoke, anxiety transparent in his tone.

'Hilary, I apologise for calling at such short notice. Maria made me come. She won't let me put this off any longer.'

'Finbar, it's been a while. Is everything okay?' She looked concerned as he strode past into the front room, his wet coat brushing against her. Hilary shivered, closed the door firmly against the wind and followed him into the room.

'I'll put the kettle on.'

'No. Can we just talk before I lose my nerve?' His hands chopped at the air for emphasis.

'Please, won't you at least sit down?' she said.

'No, I can't. Not now.' He gazed briefly at the chair. 'There's something important I have to say.' Then he lifted his face to look directly at her.

'You look terrible. What is it?' she said.

'Hilary, the last time we met, we talked briefly about your father.' He gestured to the photograph on the mantelshelf.

'Yes, I remember.' Hilary walked towards the fireplace, lifted the picture frame and drew it to her breast.

'When you told me his name, it triggered something. Then when we talked about my nightmare, that it might mean something, it worried me. When I got home that night, I had another nightmare, but this time I got to see what was waiting for me in the living room.'

'But isn't that a relief?'

'Hilary, you don't understand. The next morning it was as if a mist was lifting from my head. And the more things began to clear, the more I started to recall an incident in the late eighties on the River Foyle. A group of soldiers were killed in an explosion, opposite Carrowclare, just out beyond Ballykelly. They'd let their guard down and gone on a fishing trip. But there was a civilian on board. He was working on the boat. And I remembered the man's name was Murray Hetherington,' he said.

Hilary appeared to sink into herself. It was as though subtly she was getting smaller.

'Finbar, this is not something I find easy to talk about.'

'You've listened to me so patiently, week after week. Hilary, I need to ask you. Was it your father?'

'Yes!' She spoke emphatically. 'Daddy was murdered, a "legitimate target". He was fitting out the cabins!'

'I'm sorry, Hilary. It must have been horrific.'

'I'm not sure I'll ever fully recover from it,' she said.

'Can you tell me about it?'

'This is not how it works, Finbar. My job is to listen; yours is to talk. That's the arrangement.'

'Please, Hilary, believe me, on this occasion I need to listen. Hilary, please.'

She looked at him, then at the photograph of her father, then back at Finbar.

'I need to hear what happened to you, to your father,' he pleaded.

'I was twenty-two,' she said and then she hesitated.

'Please continue.'

'I'd just qualified in psychology at Chester,' she paused again. 'I was looking forward to coming home and spending the summer with Mummy and Daddy. I remember it was a gorgeous sunny day. Mummy and I were in the car driving back from the train station. And I switched on the radio. I was teasing Mum. She always had it set to Radio Ulster. "Just let's hear the news, then you can listen to Radio One," she said. It was Sean Rafferty's voice; I remember that distinctly. As soon as he said "explosion on the River Foyle", we both looked at each other. You know that feeling, in the pit of your stomach, like when you hear the telephone ringing and you know it's bad news?'

'Yes.' His face turned pale.

'After the police came and told us, it just didn't feel real. When we drove out to the scene, we weren't allowed beyond a certain point. That was very hard. And the worst thing, the explosion, it left us with nothing. We had no remains to bury. There was no sign of Daddy. Years later, a police officer friend said that he'd been there. All he saw was shards of wood among a swell of engine oil and blood floating out to sea. It was barbaric. Can you imagine what that does to a family, a wife, a daughter?'

'It's just too awful to take in. I'm so genuinely sorry.'

They stood in silence for a while. Finbar continually shook his head and rubbed his face with his open palm. After a few moments, Hilary spoke. 'I don't understand. Why are we talking about my father?'

'Hilary, there's something I have to tell you,' he said and paused. 'You see, after Eleanor died, I was hospitalised. You know, after being shot. It was mostly a flesh wound, painful to walk, but my leg healed. So I took the British Army to court. But I lost. I appealed and lost again. They denied all responsibility. With no evidence, no bullet, I ended up paying their legal costs as well as my own. It was a very dark and difficult time.'

'But how is this connected to my father?'

He hesitated for a moment and breathed deeply. Then he spoke. 'Shortly afterwards, I was approached by a couple of the "Boys". You know, the local IRA. They wanted to use my van. We'd lost Eleanor. I was angry and broke. The van was falling apart anyway. The insurance money would help me replace it. They came for it about half seven at night. But I delayed reporting it stolen until the next morning. The Garda found it the next day, burnt out, in Donegal.'

'Finbar, please, what are you telling me?' Her voice sounded agitated.

'My van was found in a field up at Three Trees there, near Quigley's Point in Inishowen. The rear doors, they were wide open. It was directly in line with Carrowclare on the other side of the river.'

Hilary's face drained of colour.

'That's what my nightmare was all about. Hilary, that's what was waiting for me in my living room. When I finally opened the door, it was the river. It came flooding towards me.'

'What exactly are you saying?' Hilary's voice wavered.

Finbar brought his left hand up and covered his mouth. Quickly, he took it away again. 'I believe the bomb that killed your father was detonated remotely from my van. I realise that now. That's what's been haunting me all these years.'

Hilary closed her eyes slowly. It was as if time had stopped.

'What I did was wrong,' he said.

She raised the photograph up to her face and pressed the glass of the frame against her forehead. Silence seemed to expand in the space between them.

'If I could only turn the—' Finbar said.

'He was doing a favour. That's how he was. He was kind,' she said.

'I've no right to expect …' Finbar began. 'If you'd rather I leave …' He felt his voice hanging cold in the air.

'Yes!' she said, her eyes closed. 'How could you?' she added forcefully. Then opening her eyes again, she met Finbar's gaze and screamed, 'How in God's name could you do such a thing?'

'Hilary, you've helped me, so—'

'I'd like you to leave. Now! Please leave!'

As Finbar left the room, reflected in the hall mirror he could see Hilary's eyes tracking him, rage now burning through her grief. Relieved to have finally reached the front door, he opened it, and in his haste to reach his van parked in the driveway, he left the latch ajar. In the wind it slowly opened wide onto the hall.

When Hilary heard the thump of his van door close, she reached for the porcelain container of tissues. Then, walking to the window, she watched through the blinds as his van shuddered, then stalled. On the second attempt, the whine of the ignition caught and the white exhaust plume first ballooned then dissolved into the cold night air. The vehicle reversed awkwardly into the cul-de-sac, rocking as the back wheel rolled over the kerb at her gate. She could see Finbar's contorted face looking back at her through the passenger window. For a few moments they held each other's gaze until finally he turned away and his van accelerated up the street and disappeared over the crest of the hill.

With her hands shaking, Hilary fumbled for a tissue, then abruptly gave up. With all her strength, she flung the china container against the marble of the fireplace, sending shards of porcelain exploding outwards from the cast-iron hearth. Looking down at the photograph of her smiling father, still tight in her grip, she began to wail, her cries resounding from the room, into the hallway, beyond the open front door, and out across the river.

No Strings Attached

'Guinea pigs, flamin' guinea pigs, that's what we've become,' Mal mutters to himself, returning to his desk. He drops a bundle of design lecture notes next to his in-tray, flops into his seat and exhales heavily. It is a few minutes after six o'clock. The new open-plan office has a system of bookshelf dividers around each desk, making it difficult for him to tell if he is alone.

'No, it's mushrooms. That's right, keep us in the dark and feed us the proverbial,' he says. Then he taps the return key on his laptop, bringing the screen to life. Of the thirty or so emails received today, all appeared to have been read. After scrolling the inbox, he finds a late delivery from Christine, the faculty secretary. It stands proud, in bold type, flagged red, highest priority. His eyebrows lift and he notes it was sent this evening, Friday, at five forty-five.

'Information superhighway, my ass. It's just a longer flamin' leash,' he says. He opens the email, exhales again and scans its content. 'The Head of School, Professor Robert Laverty,' Christine writes, 'wishes to remind everyone of the visit next week of Professor Trejtnar from the Prague Academy of Performing Arts.'

Christine's memo continues: 'The Dean of Faculty, Professor Susannah Lux, also invites colleagues to consider the significance and timing of this visit, both in terms of enriching the teaching programme and consolidating international synergies within the new Institute for Creative Research and Arts Practice headed by Dr Malachi Ulick Gallagher. Professor Trejtnar will be arriving at the George Best Belfast City Airport on Monday 7 April. Please see attached Professor Trejtnar's schedule.'

'No!' Mal says and flips to Monday's page in his desk diary. He finds what he is looking for among a long, handwritten list and his eyes close in slow motion. He lifts his elbows clear of the desk, both hands clasping the back of his neck, then reclines into the swivel chair, drops his head backwards and stares at the ceiling as if reading the white emulsion.

'All the responsibility, Mal, no authority and a six-thirty Monday start,' he says, having done the mental arithmetic of the Derry to Belfast car journey. Oh! And the car needs a valet, he remembers. His gaze returns to the computer screen and he opens the attached Word document. He ignores the timetable of meetings and jumps to the draft of Professor Trejtnar's teaching proposal. His face softens and he smiles for the first time all day. Trejtnar has written it himself, he guesses. The emphasis on student contact makes it obvious. Mal is heartened and ponders, perhaps, just this once it will not be the usual tedious junket. He's met his share of bloated academic dandies looking to score brownie points for their research profile, waving their international CV under your nose. Maybe this time things will be different, he hopes, and he allows himself to imagine an enthusiastic student response to Trejtnar's programme. He smiles again and reads the breakdown of the teaching plan.

WEEK 1: Day 1 – Introduction + Ice-Breakers + Lecture
Day 2 – Puppet Design – initial rough sketches
Day 3 – Puppet Design – developmental sketches
Day 4 – Self-directed student activities
Day 5 – Self-directed student activities
WEEK 2: Day 6 – Puppet Making – machining body parts
Day 7 – Puppet Making – chiselling puppet head
Day 8 – Self-directed student activities
Day 9 – Self-directed student activities
Day 10 – Closing Comments

'Jeepers! If I'd more time, I wouldn't mind doing this myself,' Mal says and for a moment is tempted to Google Trejtnar, get the low-down on his background, so to speak. It's always good to be well briefed. But he's knackered. *I'll shoot from the hip on Monday*, he tells himself. It's not the first time he's done it and he knows he can tap the adrenalin of a first encounter to conversational advantage. He logs out, switches the power button off and slumps back into his chair. Abruptly, his mobile vibrates, emits an annoying buzzing sound and spins anticlockwise on his desk. For a second, he's tempted to tip the bloody thing into the wastebasket.

'What now?' he says to the room.

'Hello … Gallagher here …'

'Oh, hi, Christine! You're not still in the office …'

'Oh, that's good …'

'No, I've just finished up. My graduate seminar ran a bit late …'

'Yes, I got your email …'

'No, no problem, I'll collect Trejtnar …'

'Yes … and the same to you. Bye-bye.'

Mal terminates the call and switches his mobile off.

'Long leash number two,' he says, dropping the phone into his bag and rising to put on his coat. Frisking the outside of his jacket, he finds his car keys, slings his bag over his shoulder and leaves the office. He descends a flight of stairs and walks out into the car park.

'Let's get outta heeagh,' he says, mimicking a New York accent.

DAY 1. INTRODUCTION – 8:15 AM

Mal yawns and rubs his face with both palms in a half-hearted attempt to freshen himself up. He's not nervous, just fidgety and eager to meet Trejtnar and get back on the road to Magee. The airport is bright and open and he likes the impression it makes, better than dour Aldergrove. The bright morning sky outside awakens a childhood memory of blue eggshell. He's about six years old. In his palm, a speckled fragment is trembling in the breeze, blown from a nest hidden in their garden hedge. 'Song thrush,' his grandfather says and quotes a verse from the Bible, Matthew's Gospel. 'Look at the birds of the air … they do not sow, nor reap …' Mal has forgotten the rest of the words, along with the faith that filled his childhood. But he has a lingering respect for the sentiment. He envies his grandfather's belief: that he could drop his worries and trust that life would carry him.

The airport lobby fills with spring sunlight, and he pictures himself delivering some Tourist Board-type spiel to Trejtnar. In his daydream, they are driving below Cave Hill, and Mal, with an easy gesture of his left hand, is referring to Napoleon's Nose and its inspiration for Swift and *Gulliver's Travels*. These little factual titbits always make for a good impression.

The sudden buzz of people steals his attention. As the throng of arrivals fan towards him, he realises he hasn't a clue what Trejtnar looks like. 'Can't see the wood for the trees' comes to mind and he stares into the middle distance and beyond. The foreground is one big, anonymous blur. *I'll spot him at a hundred yards*, he muses. *Haven't been doing this job for twenty-five years and not learned what a European professor looks like*. He blinks and a face appears in front of him: beaming insanely is his first thought; the second is it's a woman, and Mal tries to look around her, respectful, but a little impatient.

She extends an elegant hand. 'Dr Malachi Ulich Gallgaher?' she inquires, mispronouncing his name.

Mal is silent.

'Your secretary emailed me. I looked you up on your university webpage, your electronic ID card,' she elaborates.

Mal is thrown. He'd forgotten all about his electronic ID card. Externally, he is struggling to appear welcoming, capable of a relaxed intelligent conversation. But internally, he's a mess. Frantically, he tries to reconfigure, reformat his presence in front of her. Why should Trejtnar not be a woman? he berates himself. He knows loads of female academics. For God's sake, the Dean's a woman! But uncharacteristically, his brain and mouth are not in gear.

'Svetla Trejtnar,' the woman announces and squeezes his hand.

Mal is on the verge of speaking.

'You were expecting a man, weren't you?' she says and smiles playfully.

Again he hesitates.

'You were, weren't you? You can tell me. I won't bite.'

In an instant, Mal sees that she can read him. 'Well, yes,' he admits, looking sheepish but smiling. 'I do apologise, I didn't check your details. Honestly, it's really not like me,' he continues, appearing unburdened.

'I love it. I knew it,' she says. Then she claps her hands, throws her head back and laughs out loud. 'You know, it happens a lot. I like to see the surprise. Universities especially. How do they say it in English? Academic old forts?'

'I think you mean farts,' Mal says, humbled but beginning to laugh.

'Please, forgive me, I didn't mean you. I meant the university.'

They both laugh.

'Please, just call me Svetla,' she offers, shaking his hand.

'I prefer Mal myself. It's nice to meet you, Svetla. Now, let's get your bags, shall we?'

Day 1. Ice Breaking – 6:00 pm

Mal withdraws his staff swipe-card from the car park exit station, a short yellow barrier lifts and he drives off the campus onto Lawrence Hill. *The staff swipe-card, what did I tell you? Long leash number three.*

'I thought your lecture went very well, Svetla. You got a full house.'

'Oh, thank you. Yes, there were a lot more than I had expected.'

'How did this morning go? You know, with the Dean and the Head of School?'

Svetla looks at him and smiles. 'Interesting. They are, how do you say, two very different people,' she adds.

'Yes. The Dean, she likes to talk, loves jargon. I've had more two-hour monologues about the knowledge-based economy and digital storytelling than I care to remember. Her background's multimedia, or is it new-media? I can never remember which,' Mal says.

'Yes, I noticed. She did do most of the talking.'

'Yip, she's the boss. We have a saying here: she takes no prisoners.'

'Yes, I think I know what you mean. And the Head of School, what's his field?'

'Robert? Classical music, I believe, but now you've got me there, Svetla.'

'Oh, how lovely. I must talk with him more.'

Mal gets an unexpected twinge of jealousy. And from nowhere, a scene from his favourite movie, *As Good As It Gets*, pops into his head. Jack Nicholson is on a road trip and he is trying unsuccessfully to woo Helen Hunt with an array of pre-recorded car music. Helen Hunt's character is clearly unimpressed. Mal is so surprised at his feelings he almost misses his right-turn off the Culmore Road, just between the Ulster Bank and Leonardo's takeaway. Mildly flustered, he pulls up at the entrance to the Ramada Hotel complex.

'Well, Svetla, this is you. Christine has booked everything. I'll get your bags and walk you into the lobby.'

'It's fine, Mal. I can take everything from here.'

They exit either side of the car in perfect symmetry and meet at the boot in bright evening sunshine.

'Well, Mal, thank you for a very full day.'

'My pleasure. I'm sure you're exhausted, so I'll leave you to settle in. Enjoy your evening meal. They do an excellent duck, I believe.'

'Mmm, sounds lovely. Listen,' she pauses, 'I'm sure after a little nap, I'll be fine. If you're free later, why don't you join me?'

'Now, that would be *very* nice.' Mal's face lights up.

'Let's say around nine o'clock,' Svetla relaxes her finger, letting the cuff of her jacket fall back over her watch.

'Nine it is, then.' Mal replies, closing the car boot and returning to the driver's side with an imperceptible skip in his step.

'At reception, just say you're a guest of UU Magee,' he shouts over the roof of the car.

Just before nine, Mal enters through the rotating doors of the hotel. He's wearing his shades as he calls them. Svetla is already waiting for him in the lobby. She looks wonderfully refreshed and is dressed in a relaxed dark-green evening dress. Understated but elegant, he thinks. Mal has changed into his favourite pair of special-occasion jeans and a fresh shirt.

'Lovely dress,' Mal announces, trying not to sound too enthusiastic. He removes his sunglasses and slips them over the top button of his open-neck shirt.

'Thank you.' Svetla reaches forward to touch the fabric of his shirt. 'Irish linen, such a beautiful material,' she adds.

'Magee's, Donegal town. They sell the odd little gem. They have a women's department, too, I believe,' he says.

'Do they? And is Donegal far from here?'

'Well, there's Donegal the town, where Magee's Clothing is based, and then there's Donegal the county. The county's just up the road.'

'Really? I've heard the landscape is something special.'

'I'm sure I could arrange a little sight-seeing,' Mal suggests.

'I'd like that.'

'Leave it with me,' he says.

'Thank you, Mal.'

'Perhaps we should go in?' Mal gestures towards the doors leading to the restaurant.

'Yes. There's a table waiting.'

'Don't know about you, Svetla, but I'm famished.'

DAY 3. PUPPET DESIGN – 2:00 PM

A motorbike pulls up loudly in front of the campus design studios. Mal looks out through an open window and sees Billy Carlin the design technician switch off the engine and dismount. He watches as Svetla, the pillion passenger, swings her long legs free of the leather seat, stands upright and removes a black helmet. She shakes her auburn hair loose, turns and looks out across the River Foyle. One floor above, Mal can clearly hear their voices.

'Thanks, Billy. That was a wonderful trip. You live in a very beautiful part of the world. I hadn't realised just how close the university is to the coast.'

'You're more than welcome, Svetla. It's all part of the official departmental itinerary. If the weather's fine, Mal asks me to invite our braver guests out on a little lunchtime spin along the river. Blow the cobwebs off them, Mal says. You wouldn't believe how many external examiners I have softened up on this bike,' he says and laughs.

'Oh, I believe you. I think my cobwebs have been truly blown off. Thanks for a lovely tour. Perhaps we should go inside. Mal and the students will be waiting.'

Mal watches them disappear under the canopy of the front entrance and briefly daydreams. He imagines himself dressed in black leather, Billy's bike roaring under him. Svetla sits behind, clinging to him like a limpet. His thinning red hair is blowing freely, licking at her locks. They're like a flame in the wind, the open road rolling out far in front of them, on into infinity.

When Svetla and Billy enter, Mal turns to face them. The room is long and thin with a high ceiling – a design studio of sorts – fragmented into six corrals providing thirty workstations. Each workstation has chest-high pin-board dividers forming discreet creative environments, festooned with photocopies, collages, clippings of typefaces, prints of illustrations, CD covers, the standard party shots, art photography, images of sculpture and lots of sketches of puppets. The students are milling about, clearly waiting for the design critique to start.

Mal has arranged for them to pin their design drawings in a sequence along the west wall of the studio. It's an impressive display and he is proud of their efforts. He acknowledges Svetla and Billy, exchanging a few muffled greetings as they reach him. When everyone is ready, he stands up to address the class.

'So, everyone. Just to recap on what Svetla was saying before lunch. By end of business today, we're aiming to confirm that your designs are on the right track. You'll continue self-directed until next week. Then, with Billy's help, we can start the process of making our puppets. Billy's going to sit in on this design crit in case any production issues arise. Is everyone clear on that? Anyone have any questions?'

'Mal, I just wondered. Will you be making a puppet yourself?' a student asks, clearly joking.

'Very good, very good. Much as I'd like to, Simon, I think I'm fairly tied up as it is. Don't you think?' Mal says.

A mock groan ripples through the class.

'Right, then. Assuming we have no further burning questions, I think we'll work from the left. So, Nicole. If you don't mind, I think we'll start with you. In your own time, just you take us through your character designs.'

Day 7. Puppet Making – 10:00 am

Outside the new campus library building, Mal and Svetla are sitting on a bench overlooking Lough Foyle, in the shade of a row of cherry blossoms. They are sipping at take-away coffees.

'You are good at what you do, Mal. Very good, I would say. But are you happy?' Svetla asks, cradling her cup in both palms, warming her hands.

'What makes you ask?' Mal takes a drink.

'Well, they have you doing three jobs. You are teaching, you are managing and you're Head of Research. That's a lot.'

'I know. You're dead right.'

'And the name of your research institute, Creative Research and Arts Practice, it's CRAP for short? Even with my limited English, I spotted that.' She starts laughing.

Mal laughs along with her.

'Committees, academic committees,' he acknowledges.

'University research, really, it's all about generating income. I'm sure you're bringing in more money than they're paying you. What about *you*? Do you find time for Mal?'

'I'll tell you better than that. My initials, Malachi Ulick Gallagher, it's MUG for short. Sometimes they have me so wrapped-up in red tape, I barely have wriggle room.'

They sit in silence for a while taking lazy sips of their coffee. 'What was your first love? I mean, creatively speaking?' Svetla asks.

'Sculpture, would you believe?'

'Really? Me, too. So what happened?'

'Life, I suppose. One day I was this eager young artist, in love, full of ideas and plans. Then, the next time I look, I'm this divorced, dusty academic, pushing paper. It's odd, but increasingly I've felt like a doomed character in some dark fairytale.' Mal wiggles the fingers of his free hand in mock imitation of a spectre.

'You know, you should just get a giant pair of scissors and cut all the bureaucratic strings, one by one.' Svetla makes little snipping movements with her fingers.

'You don't happen to know where I can get a pair of these scissors?' he inquires playfully.

'I think I might know someone.'

'And then what would I do?'

'Write your own script, Mal. It can be done. Really, you can just do it.'

'Svetla, I'm fifty.'

'Mal, I'm thirty-eight. You might not think it now, but three years ago I was quite ill. If I can do it, so can you.'

'God, I'm so sorry. I didn't realise. Was it serious?'

'I had breast cancer. Thankfully, it was non-invasive and the surgery was successful. I'm fine now. I'm managing. It's my life; I've just learned to take as much control of it as I can.'

'Christ!' Mal sighs.

They sit silently for a while, watching the clouds drift above the river.

'Let's walk for a bit, before we meet Billy and the students,' he says.

'Yes, that would be nice.'

They are both standing at the check-in desk in the airport. Svetla has her bags and Mal is carrying a small cardboard box. It rests in his forearms like a baby. He assumes it's a puppet, but he hasn't had a chance to peek inside.

'You have the students all fired up now,' he says. 'The trip to Prague in October came as a complete surprise to them,' he adds.

'Yes, well, it's perfect, don't you think? Your students design and make the puppets, and ours string them, create the costumes and the performances around the characters. I'm really looking forward to their visit. You're coming, too?'

'I wouldn't miss it, Svetla.'

She offers her documents to the check-in clerk and drops her bags on the conveyor belt. The digital-weight indicator spools numbers until it settles at 16.3 kilos. Mal prepares to pass her the box, but she places her hand firmly on the lid.

'No, Mal. This is my gift; this is for you. Now, promise me you won't open it until you are back in the car. I'm not one for goodbyes, so I'm going to head straight through.' She gestures towards the security gates.

'Svetla, really, there's no need, this is a—'

'Mal, I've had a wonderful time. Everyone has been very good to me, you especially.' She leans forward and kisses him on both cheeks.

What with the smell of lipstick, perfume, the sudden intimacy and the gift, he's stunned. Mal just stands there as she walks towards departure. She waves at him and he tries to wave back, but with the box still resting on his forearms, he can only wriggle his fingers.

'See you in six months,' he calls after her.

'There is a note in the box,' she replies and then abruptly disappears behind the opaque glass partition of the departure lounge.

Back in the car, Mal lifts the lid off the box and peels back the layers of wrapping until he sees a little wooden face staring back at him. It's swathed in white like a newborn child. Despite the sculptural weight of the carved features, he recognises himself, the receding hairline, the long nose and whimsical eyes. He laughs out loud.

'Svetla, you're good, you're very good,' he says. Then he finds the note placed under its wooden hand. Admiring the workmanship, he lifts the limb by the elbow, intrigued by its mechanical articulation. On the envelope, he reads, 'No strings attached.'

He opens it and removes a postcard. It's a moody photograph of Prague, the Vltava River and the Charles Bridge at night. On the back, Svetla has written: *This is Mal. Please look after him. When you visit in October, I'll help you attach his strings. Write your own script! Svetla.*

'Yes!' Mal shouts, punching the air through the open car window.

CIRCULAR BREATHING

'Keep her lit!' Conal always said just before the singing stopped. Then he would set his Guinness on the hearth, and with sleight-of-hand, his false teeth would disappear, replaced by a tin harmonica between his lips. The melody of his party piece, *Waltzing Matilda,* would grow in strength until it filled the room. There would be a quiver to the notes of the chorus and a tear would form in his left eye.

And with this familiar scene began Brigitte's love of music and its power to draw the past into the company of the present.

Now, twenty years later, among the audio files stored on Brigitte's laptop, were the liquid heartbeat of her unborn niece, children reciting their ten-times tables and the call of a curlew over Inishowen. As she recorded the ebb and flow of the shoreline, she wondered if within the rhythm of the waves there remained an echo of the seabed.

'Let's put you under Nature/RiverFoyle/Ten,' Brigitte said and stored her sample. The battery symbol was low and a dialog-box prompted her that she was running on reserve.

'Yes, I get the message,' she said as the screen began to function in a weaker mode. She pressed shutdown, then closed the laptop and slipped it into her backpack. Standing upright at the shore's edge, she faced the breeze, her thick dyed hair, a mix of red and green, trailing behind her like seaweed.

* * *

Settling into a seat on the Lough Swilly Bus, Bulayu fiddled with his MP3 player. He started humming, half-singing *Arms Around The World*. So as not to spill his gear onto the seat beside him, he propped a stiff canvas bag vertically between his knees. To a fishing man's eye it might have contained a rod and tackle, but it didn't. Better that it looked inconspicuous anyway, he thought.

Bulayu was now feeling the effects of almost thirty hours in the air. He was thinking of Lily and how she had left Ireland over sixty years before. Now that he was at last on her home soil, he was determined to stay awake. And as the bus approached her birthplace, the landscape began to refresh him, its lush greenness so rare at home. She had been right, though. He had noticed that when he spoke, people did warm to his accent. Women especially, their faces turning like flowers towards a southern sun. Just as he took a paperback from his jacket pocket, the driver pulled up at a stop and some extra passengers boarded. After a few moments, the bus drove off again and an old man shuffled to a stop in the aisle. He turned to face Bulayu and then sat down beside him. After a while, he seemed to take an interest in Bulayu's baggage.

'Where are you from, son?' he said.

'Oh, hi!' Bulayu unplugged his right earpiece. Then he flashed the cover of his book and said, 'Australia, mate. My name's Bulayu.'

The man's eyes narrowed as he read the title, '*Inside Black Australia – An Anthology of Aboriginal Poetry*.' Then his brow relaxed again and his face softened. 'Well now.' He coughed. 'Your name, that's a rare one. But as my mother always said, a face is like a book. Looking at you again, I believe I can read it in you. Michael, my name's Michael. Welcome to Inishowen.'

He offered his hand.

'Cheers, mate,' Bulayu said. And in Michael's knuckled grasp, he sensed a life working the land.

'What brings you all the way here? Not the fishing, surely?' Michael cleared his throat, bringing on another cough. He gestured to the bag.

'No, not at all. It was my nana. She was born here. She passed away just last year. When she was crook – you know, sick – I promised I'd make a special visit.'

'I'm sorry to hear that now.'

106

Bulayu rubbed his palm down the length of his book, flattening the spread of pages.

'Do you mind if I have a wee peek?' Michael pointed at a poem.

'No worries.' Bulayu handed him the paperback.

Michael raised his glasses up onto his forehead and drew the page close to his face. 'Ood— Oodgeroo Noonuccal,' he said, enunciating slowly. Then he glanced back at Bulayu for reassurance.

'Not bad, mate. Oodgeroo: that's the poet's name; it means old. From the Noonuccal tribe, she was the first Aboriginal poet to get published. Back in the sixties.'

Michael's eyes returned to the page again and he read aloud.

'The past. Let no-one say the past is dead. The past is all about us and within. I know this little now, this accidental present is not the all of me.' Then he paused. The bus rounded a wide bend and he leaned into Bulayu's shoulder.

'Speaking of the past, that's my old school.' He pointed with the spine of the book out beyond the dirt and the rain on the window.

'Hollybush Primary, we all had to bring turf for the morning fire. Miss Quigley, she loved art, you know. Always showing us books on painting.'

Bulayu could see a long single-storey building attached to a two-storey house. It had a fresh coat of white paint. There was a child's bike lying on the ground at the front door. It appeared to be a family home now. But he thought that he recognised it from a dog-eared sepia print he'd seen hanging from the door of Lily's room. She'd built herself a makeshift sleep-out on their veranda.

* * *

Sitting at a booth next to a wall of glass in the university library, Brigitte struggled to concentrate. She was reading a book on prehistoric music and came across a passage referring to a technique known as circular breathing. It read:

A means by which the player is able to produce a continuous sound without being compelled to stop and take a breath, it is generally accepted … that circular breathing was commonly used to play many instruments throughout the ancient world.

Distracted by the play of light outside, she raised her eyes. She could see a line of cherry blossoms. But her gaze drifted out and beyond the campus, along the grass bank overlooking the city and down to the stretch of water where the Foyle met Inishowen. A sudden, sharp rap on the window made her jump and she refocused to see her friend Catherine's bright smile. Brigitte laughed and pointed towards the snack bar and mimed drinking a coffee. But Catherine tapped her watch and imitated the posture of her tubby professor. Now they both laughed silently on either side of the glass. After a series of exaggerated expressions and page-flicking in her diary, they agreed to meet on Friday and Catherine left, taking the path leading down the grass bank to the Arts building. Now unsettled, Brigitte gathered her things and climbed the stairs to the computer lab on the top floor.

'Happy days,' she said, seeing there were no emails in her mailbox. Anyway, her tutorial feedback had been positive; she'd passed her initial *Viva*. Besides, from the third floor, the view of the river was overwhelming. It was too good a day to be indoors. She nodded at the IT technician, shouldered her bag and made her way down again, through the revolving doors and out into the afternoon sun.

* * *

Bulayu was walking up the hill to Iskaheen, his bag across his back, his senses attuned to this new world he now found himself in. He mulled over what Lily had said.

'Assuming it's still there, take the lane past Harkin's shop. It's a gentle climb. Check for the red squirrels in the woods at the top of the hill. Bring them some nuts and seeds, mind. You can leave them on the old stump in the clearing. Then head back out onto the lane again and follow it until you come to a fork in the road. Be sure and take a right. The view will unfold. It's a lovely way to arrive.'

He heard it before he saw it, a high-pitched chattering as though rebuking him from above. Then it was away, speeding across the canopy, a fiery-brown shadow and a length of bushy tail.

'Lily, they're still here,' he said.

Later, out on the road, responding to a plaintive 'peeiou' call, he scanned the sky for the slow flap of broad wings and found a buzzard circling, wing tips splayed out, soaring above the hillside. Then it hovered. And in lowering his gaze, Bulayu noticed a small spire above the tree line. He began walking towards it. As Iskaheen Chapel came into view, his eyes were drawn to the marble plaque high on the graveyard wall.

EOGHAN, PRINCE OF INIS EOGHAIN, SON OF NIALL OF THE
NINE HOSTAGES,
DIED OF GRIEF, AT THE DEATH OF HIS BROTHER, IN 465,
BAPTISED BY PATRICK IS BURIED HERE.

There was a rusted gate and he eased a chain from a metal peg, letting it fall slack. He pushed and there was a loud squeak. An ivy-clad archway framed the view spreading before him. The yew trees and tilting gravestones led him to a vibrant patch of yellow, low on the ground.

'You'll recognise it by its dark-green, heart-shaped leaves and brilliant-yellow flowers. The celandine is a flower of the sun,' Lily had told him. 'Its petals stay closed on a dull day. But in bright light, especially in the morning, they unfold. He loved the sun; so go on a bright day, and when you find some, place a bunch on his grave. Bulayu, will you promise me that?'

'Of course, Nana, I promise. He'll have a pillow of celandine as soon as I arrive,' Bulayu told her. Then he'd squeezed the loose flesh of her forearm and she had relaxed back into the pillow, her fine white hair still holding a wave. Gradually, her breath had become less laboured and she had slipped into a light sleep.

* * *

Brigitte was walking the shoreline path from Moville to Green-castle. She felt that sense of lightness and promise unique to spring. The river was calm. The coastline was a mix of sheltered coves and sandy beaches. Shells and strands of bladderwrack lay strewn across her path, crunching and slithering underfoot. She passed three Shetland ponies grazing along the edges of a chain-link fence. Wind-sculpted shrubs bordered an abandoned deer farm. Ferns, finding their sap again, had formed frothy banks on either side. Entering a shady overhang, she smelled blackthorn blossom. Brigitte raised her hand to touch the petals and was surprised by a distinctive 'churp, churp, churp'. Unmistakeable: it was the chorus of a song thrush.

She looked up over the next rise and her thoughts drifted to the harbour two kilometres away. There, she hoped to record the seagulls as the fishing vessels unloaded. Already, she could hear the drone of the ferry crossing the puckered mouth of the Foyle.

* * *

After leaving the graveyard, Bulayu made his way back down the hill again. He thumbed a lift to the spot out along the river where Lily had told him to go. A crow flapped lazily above him as he unzipped the canvas bag and withdrew a length of wood. He allowed for the forward creep of the waves as he placed one end on the sand, the coarse grain warm to his bare feet. He had that leggy leanness so typical of his ancestors, but his skin was not black. Lowering himself onto a smooth rock, he raised his right knee to support his elbow and stretched out his left leg. Then he rested the length of wood against the tip of his left foot. He began by filling his lungs through to the diaphragm. And Lily's words drifted back to him.

'They sent me his paintings after all these years. Bulayu, it's so good to see them, to know he never forgot. Ireland in those days, it was so easy to have your future taken from you. Society interfered, just like here in Australia. Except for your mother; it was her past they stole. To know that his feelings remained, it's lovely to read his longing through the spread of his paint.'

Lily's hand travelled over the raised pigment and continued until it left the edges of the painting. She winced and from the side of her bed she attempted to lift a long, gift-wrapped object.

'What are you doing, Nana? You'll strain yourself.' Bulayu took hold of the item and placed it on the bed.

'I need you to tell him my story,' Lily whispered, unwrapping the tissue to reveal the traditional markings. Her shaking clasp drew Bulayu's hand onto the wooden shaft.

'You are all I have now, Bulayu.'

Bulayu could see from the craftsmanship that Yarramalong had made it. He was skilled at releasing the rich, resonant sound from the blood-wood gum. His earthy pigments described the sacred symbols in X-ray style. The crow was there, the totem of the Wiradjuri, along with a fish, a kangaroo and the rainbow serpent, the mother of life.

'Let him hear you, let him hear you sing up our story into life,' Lily told him. Then her fingers tapped Bulayu's abdomen, part in blessing and part in farewell.

On the shoreline, Bulayu began by flushing the didgeridoo with water to enrich its voice. Then with loose lips, he started to call up the droning sound, his mouth working like an airbag, pushing his breath down the length of the instrument. Periodically, he snatched short breaths through his nose, his abdomen pumping like bellows. Steadily, the note varied in rhythm and moved from a slow growling into the dog bark, then at intervals came the kookaburra laugh, followed after some minutes by the kangaroo hop. He prolonged the phrases and began weaving the sounds from earlier in the day: the buzzard call, the squirrel chatter, their voices blending until, engrossed by his own music, Bulayu became entranced.

'That's so beautiful,' Brigitte said as she stumbled in disbelief at the scene in front of her.

Startled by the sheer clarity and projection of her voice, Bulayu jolted backwards, his lips missing the mouthpiece by some distance. The hypnotic sound stopped completely.

'Crikey!' Bulayu turned towards Brigitte. 'You scared the shit out me!'

'I'm sorry, but you're such a sight for sore eyes,' she said, standing on the path behind him.

* * *

After travelling back to Derry, they spent the rest of the day together in Sandino's bar. Small and narrow, it backed on to the bus station. Bulayu played with a musician in the corner, a fiddler from London.

'That's some craic,' someone said to him, pointing at the images on the didgeridoo. But as the crowd faded, Brigitte invited him back to her room in Barry Street. There, she recorded him playing. Talking into the mic on her laptop, he explained the symbolism of the sounds and the phrasing. When he finished, she asked him to play the whole piece again, this time uninterrupted. When he finished, they opened a few beers and shared the remnants of a takeaway pizza.

'So, tell me. You were saying Lily was your grandmother?' she said, chewing on a piece of crust.

'No, not really.'

'Oh, can I have them?' Brigitte pointed to the black olives piled on his plate.

'Sure, fire away.'

'I'm confused.' She guzzled on a bottle of Miller.

'Well, she was always around. So we started calling her Nana. It just stuck. She became family.'

'So you are Aboriginal, then? It's just, I mean, you're not … black.'

'I'm from the Wiradjuri tribe. We're from the Murrumbidgee River basin in New South Wales. My name, Bulayu, it means from two places. Mum chose it as a thank you to Lily.'

'Aboriginal words, they sound so distinctive.'

Bulayu gave a brief nod of appreciation.

'So your name, then, is it Irish?' he said, swallowing a mouthful of beer.

'Well, Mum is German and Dad is Irish. Brigid was some kind of Celtic symbol of spring, a pagan goddess, I think. That is, until the Christians got hold of her, turned her into a bloody saint. Brigitte, it's just the German version.'

'Nice.' He took a long throaty drink. Bulayu felt relaxed now and was beginning to enjoy his fantasies, unconcerned if she could read them in his eyes. They were sitting on the floor, and every few minutes, he'd catch a glimpse of her thigh. Jesus, she's some Sheila, he thought.

'But your skin colour, what's the story?' she inquired.

'It sounds odd, but you can be white and still be Aboriginal.'

'A white Aboriginal? Now that sounds interesting.' Then she smiled, leaned forward and kissed him.

* * *

The next day, in the dim light of Sandino's, Bulayu watched as Brigitte approached the bar. Her hair was gathered over her right shoulder, thick as a horsetail. She wore a linen dress. A single zip described the line of her back from her shoulders down to the base of her spine. Raising her heels, the muscles from her calves up to her buttocks clenched slightly. With both elbows, she leaned on the counter and ordered her drinks.

'Guinness and a Smithwicks, John, when you're ready.'

'Soon as I saw you through the window, I had the glass in my hand. I'll drop them down to you. Is that you in the corner?' John raised an eyebrow and gave a wry grin.

'Ah, stop, will you? We only met yesterday.' But she couldn't help a smile spread across her face.

'What's wrong with us local lads, then?' John joked, placing the half-poured Guinness on the counter to settle.

'Ah, now, John.' She turned and walked back to her table.

'Just ignore him,' pleaded Brigitte as she sat facing Bulayu.

Looking past each other, they waited on their pints. Bulayu had assumed they'd sit side by side. He'd even made room for her. But after the intimacy of the previous night, when his eyes met hers, he felt self-conscious.

A few minutes later, John approached the table, serving the Guinness first and then placing the Smithwicks in front of Bulayu.

'You know what they say about fiery-haired women?' he said, winking at Bulayu.

'Will you stop?' Brigitte feigned mock frustration.

She tracked Bulayu's hand as he raised the pint to his lips and supped generously. She took in his brown eyes, how his dark pupils expanded as he looked at her. Gorgeous. His awkwardness, his transparency, she knew the moment she saw him at the water's edge, heard the didgeridoo, saw his flat belly and his strong legs that she'd wanted him.

'Last night, you said something about Aboriginal kids being taken away.' The tone of her voice sounded strangely at odds with her thoughts.

'Yeah. Fair-skinned kids were taken from their families and fostered into white ones. It stopped around the sixties, I think. Anyway, my mum, she was one of them.'

'And Lily?'

'Well, in the eighties, she worked with a support group trying to link up the separated kids with their Aboriginal families.'

'And your mum, did she find her family?'

'Yeah, in the end she did. But it was very traumatic. Lily, she somehow understood. She was a big help for us all, really. Especially through the whole reunion thing.'

Bulayu turned towards the window and narrowed his eyes as if focusing on something out on the far bank of the river.

Brigitte placed her hand on his forearm and stroked the

fine, sun-bleached hairs on his skin. They appeared almost golden. 'Can I ask you something?' she said.

'Crikey, you're one nosey parker,' he joked, returning his attention to her. They both gave a shy laugh and raised their pints and supped generously. He swallowed. 'Well? What is it you want to know?' He placed his drink back on the table.

'Lily's special friend, the person you've travelled all this way to pay her respects to?'

'Yeah. What about him?'

'Do you know did he ever play the harmonica?'

'Yeah, I think he did. Why?'

MARTY'S GOSPEL

I have to tell you about last Thursday. I don't fully understand how it happened myself. But then, that's the way I am about a lot of things. You know, like how a computer works, where my thoughts come from, what is this thing called life. Recently, I heard a guy on Radio Foyle, some expert on biology. I didn't catch his name. He said the essential ingredients of life feeding the heartwood of a tree are still present in a fallen branch. Although the tree lives, the fallen branch is dead. Science, he said, still hasn't solved the mystery of it all. Now that did surprise me. I thought with something so fundamental, the experts had it sussed long ago.

Anyway, back to last Thursday. It was a day just like any other. I was taking my tea break at eleven o'clock. We have a microwave at work and I always enjoy a wee fruit scone. After it's warmed up a bit, I cut it at an angle and drop in a couple of squares of butter. They melt beautifully that way. Then I grab a seat at one of the tables, just behind the children's section, and read for fifteen minutes or so. You're probably thinking tabloid, but you'd be wrong. You see, I adore books, always have. As a boy, I was lucky. At home, we had books in every room of the house, including the loo. Their subjects ranged from literature and history to the arts. My dad was an obsessive reader. And he got the love of books from *his* dad. They both grew up in Belfast, you see, during the era of the old Smithfield Market. For second-hand books, Smithfield was a great cavern of a place. The shelves would be so crammed; the books were often stacked in rickety piles or stuffed into boxes waiting to be discovered. My dad said it was a real treasure trove.

He told me how, as a schoolboy after the war, he'd often go in to stare at the columns of books. One day, his head still brimming with details from a science lesson, he had imagined they were soaring stalagmites. It was as if up there in the vaulted ceiling some hidden stalactite was dripping pages down onto the book piles. He said it was like he could see their meaning accumulate, slowly calcify before his eyes. Like some devoted pilgrim, he remembered standing in awe at the monumental scale of all the books, as though he were looking at the paintings in some great cathedral.

I remember our little library at home; it started with the Encyclopaedia Britannica. My dad inherited the 1950 edition. It sat in pride of place, on two shelves to the right of the chimneybreast. And barely audible above our ticking clock, I imagined I could hear something. It was difficult to describe the sound, not quite music, more like a draught whispering through a harmonica. All twenty-five volumes seemed to be exhaling a faint melody along their scales of subjects. Each volume held about a thousand pages. Printed on very fine paper, similar to the type used in Bibles, for me, their contents had an air of reverence. That's when I developed this feeling that books somehow contained the energy of a gospel. Back in the fifties, the layout of encyclopaedias was mostly text, with the odd black-and-white photograph or illustration. And yet, I remember being impressed with the regimented columns of text. Their architecture seemed part of a grand plan, like the formal gardens of some grand Elizabethan house.

So, back to last Thursday. I was shelving the modern fiction section. I work in the library on Foyle Street. No surprise there, you're thinking. Well, for me, stacking is easily the best part of the job. Afterwards, I like to walk between the walls of books and just listen. I fancy I hear them mumbling away about their contents. I imagine it's a bit like a graveyard, the voices of the dead percolating up through the moist soil. Except, I think with the voices in a book, the reader becomes like a medium of sorts, bringing them back to life. Sounds crazy, I know. But I'm convinced if you trundle your finger along a shelf of books, you can release their individual notes, like the keys of a piano. Sometimes I find if I linger at a particular book, it resonates, vibrating out through my hand, along the length of my arm until its timbre sounds in my head. That's exactly what happened last Thursday. I had just finished shelving and I rested my index finger on the spine of the last book. It turned out to be a novel by Paul Auster, *The Music of Chance*. The urge to pick it up was overwhelming. So I did. And as I said at the start, I decided to take my eleven o'clock tea break.

'The usual, Marty?' Mary the tea lady asked.

'That'll hit the spot,' I replied.

Well, the scone didn't last long, I can tell you. So I settled into reading and was happily supping at my mug of tea. I'm quite a fast reader, and when I checked, I saw I was nearing the end of chapter one. If you want to know, I was between pages forty-one and forty-two. It's strange, now that I think of it, that's my age, too. It was one of those moments when you just get lost in a book. I saw a documentary recently about John McGahern, where he said that as a child he would often get so engrossed in reading that his sisters would try all sorts of pranks in order to wake him out of the book. Well, that's just the way it was. I was totally engrossed.

Then out of the bloody blue, no warning, no pangs, no anything. Just wallop! I had this friggin' heart attack. I died right bang in the process of reading.

And I thought that was it – until you came along.

RE-IMAGINING FISH

Now that the days were getting longer, Karin's skin, always a light olive, had begun to darken. The temperature was 18°C, good for Donegal in late April. She was wearing a yellow bikini under a blue linen dress. Everything she needed for the day was in a white cotton bag beside her: a beach towel, homemade salad sandwiches and a large bottle of Evian. A novel and a slender finger of Kinder chocolate were just visible through the bag's tangle of handles. In the car glove-pocket there was a balding tennis ball. Shannon, her golden retriever, was sitting in the back seat. As Karin drove towards the coast, she sang along with the CD, '... *the homes of Donegal.*'

Now and then she glanced at Shannon through the rear-view mirror. His strong, gentle head rested on the rim of the open rear window. Karin smiled as Shannon's jowls flapped and his ears blew behind him in the breeze. She simply adored these relaxed moments with her dog; his companionship and his easy loyalty. 'Swoo Swoh' she whistled and chuckled to see his left ear twitch and his brow wrinkle in response. Life was good, she thought.

The sky was a clear blue, and if Portsalon beach proved deserted, she pictured herself swimming naked. Shannon had learned to hold her swimsuit in his mouth and paddle alongside her. Space was the thing Karin loved about Donegal. Even its bleak stretches of bog appealed to her. It was a world away from the forests of Bavaria, a relief to have left Regensburg, the town where she'd grown up. Its narrow streets, its brooding architecture were now just a vague memory.

Every few minutes, she glanced out and along the coastline. The road began to rise steadily up to follow the curve of the headland. She could now see the salmon farm below, its elliptical cages set in rhythmic patterns close to the shore. A solitary figure stood silhouetted next to the last cage. And for a moment she contemplated the life of a farmed fish, then shivered, proclaiming in her mind that all fish should swim free. The water appeared calm, but she knew beneath its surface, as always, a strong undertow remained. She began to anticipate the feel of water on her skin, the sensation of gliding just feet below. Testing the swimming distance of her breath had become a regular challenge. The sea, she felt, teemed with life: seaweed, crabs and all sorts of fish she couldn't name. Once, while floating on her back, a seal pup had approached. But for Karin the highlight had been a bottle-nosed dolphin that occasionally visited the Lough. Just inches away, her fingers had strained to reach its glistening skin. If there was a single element that carried meaning for Karin it was water, and Ireland was surrounded by it.

Then there had been that wonderful summer solstice. It was the year Claudia, her daughter, was conceived. She had attracted Brendan's attention by the playful rise and fall of her buttocks in the waves. Eventually, when he had entered the water, they had made love. She had relished the feel of sand biting into her skin, her bum and shoulders stinging as she had arched her spine. She had felt the sea and their bodies blend as one. The rhythm of the waves had seemed to wash everything from her mind. As a young girl she had remembered seeing an erotic Japanese print. And it had suddenly flooded her consciousness. She had become the woman in the image by Hokusai, *Dream of the Fisherman's Wife*. Karin sensed the octopus, its tentacles probing her ears, her mouth. She felt it slithering and sliding over her breasts, her belly and her thighs.

The shadow of a seagull skimmed like a ribbon of charcoal across a granite boulder, graceful but sudden. And with all the energy of spring in its legs, a startled lamb bolted. Assisted by the steep incline of the field, it leaped clear of the tangle of wire and posts that bordered its world. Abruptly, the animal was out on the road. Confused but standing, it stared straight ahead.

When Karin's car rounded the bend, what she saw suddenly in front of her was the bewildered face of the lamb, its gaping mouth and pink tongue moving silently. Fifteen years of driving had no influence over her instinctive decision to swerve. Unrestrained, Shannon was thrown to the left, then forward, plunging between the seats. Karin reached out to save him. The front wheel hit a pothole on the driver's side. The steering spun hard to the right. She made to grab for the dog's collar and stamped vigorously on the brakes. It was her only control as they sailed over the edge of the headland.

The lamb paused a moment and then bleated. Without looking back, it ran around the bend and down the road.

* * *

Brendan pressed the eject button and removed his daughter's Snow Patrol CD. He replaced it with THE BEST OF PAUL BRADY. The first track, *The World Is What You Make It*, started to play. Rain fell. Not heavy, but enough to set the wipers to intermittent. He resisted the urge to turn them on and watched as the amber streetlights blended with the droplets. Slowly, his view of the City Hotel dissolved, trickled and then flowed to the bottom of the windscreen. Lyrics seeped out through the speakers. He wasn't listening.

'For God's sake what's keeping her?' he said, checking the clock on the dashboard. Drawn by the pull of the river, he looked to his left and watched its dark weight slide by. Almost instantly, his breathing became laboured.

'Okay, here it comes again,' he said. Patricia, his psychologist, had recommended he 'breathe in slowly through the nose and then out through the mouth'. Even so, the familiar sequence of images returned and spooled rapidly in his mind.

Karin is driving their old blue Escort. And in the back seat, Shannon, their devoted dog, is asleep. They are on the high approach overlooking Lough Swilly. Brendan imagines the scene as the car leaves the road, making a sweeping arc in its plunge towards the water. He feels the impact of the powerful entry and watches their frantic convulsions as instinct takes over, their limbs scrambling for air. Then the ice-cold water engulfs them. Their movements are reduced to slow motion. Karin's long hair is suddenly weightless, swirling up and behind her head. Shannon's powerful bark is transformed into bubbles scrambling towards the surface. He imagines CDs, pens, perhaps a novel, gently spiralling upwards. The weight of the engine drags them to the bottom. He conjures up a world increasingly dark and murky, of rocks and sediment, a rusting fishing vessel covered by a thin aquatic fur. And when life leaves them both and their bodies have become bone-cold husks, his mind's eye seeks out Karin's final, vacant stare.

Tonight, almost three years on, Brendan's recurring vision is no less vivid, but his hyperventilation is less intense. Yet one thing remains. The current he rides in his head, it conveys only death. Never once does he imagine the presence of fish.

After the accident, he received no full explanation. Only Shannon was found, wedged and contorted in the footwell. The eyewitness evidence of a salmon farmer and the twisted waterlogged wreckage of the car offered some understanding. The opened driver's window suggested how the tide might have stolen her away. Ever since, Brendan remained an island: inward, gloomy, inaccessible.

'Karin, *wo bist du*? Karin, where did you go?' he said.

His thoughts drifted back to their early years together, to her love of the Irish coastline and the sea. He recalled her swimming out into the waves until she became a shimmering blur, bobbing and waving on the surface as he sat barefoot in the sand, reading a book. Often she teased him. The idea of Irishmen, surrounded by the sea, unable to swim amused her. Coming from landlocked Bavaria, she was determined he would learn to trust the sea, discover the life-giving force of water.

'Brendan, don't be mud on the stick,' she had laughed.

'A stick-in-the-mud,' he had corrected her. And he remembered her dragging him, gripping both his wrists. He must have looked silly as he limped gingerly over pebbles and shells towards the shoreline.

Brendan switched on the ignition, turned the heater to max and the fan to three. He directed the air vents to the windscreen and his feet. The screen began to clear in mushrooming patches from the bottom up.

'Jesus, it's cold. Claudia, where the hell are you?' He fumbled for a cigarette. Tapping one free from the packet, he lit it and inhaled, filling his lungs in one deep draw. Seconds later, directed by his upper lip, the smoke fanned down and over his right shoulder. As he opened his window to clear the air, he knew he was due an earful of complaint.

'Brendan,' Claudia always called him by his name, never Dad. 'Haven't you seen the ads on TV? Do you want to see your fifties?' she always said.

Brendan took another drag.

'Fuck it! Today of all days, half past one in the bloody morning and I'm sitting here freezing my balls off!'

* * *

'You'll be here until the end of semester at least?' Claudia inquired, reading her boyfriend's face.

'Of course. Don't worry, my student placement lasts until the end of May. Once I transfer my results over to the *Fachhochschule* in Augsburg, end of June, I'm all yours,' Stefan said.

Claudia clung to him, the right side of her face pressing into the sweat of his T-shirt. She loved his tallness, his strong German-ness.

'Did the manager pay you yet? It's just that it's getting late and my dad, he'll be pissed off. Ever since my mum, he hates waiting. I'd really like you two to meet.'

'Okay, let's go. The band can sort me out tomorrow. The crowd was magic, though. Wow! I feel fantastic!' Stefan punched the air.

They held each other, her arms under his coat, his eyes taking in her open face.

'We really need to go. It's getting on for two. We'd better get down there.'

Stefan kissed her on the cheek and grabbed a blue plastic bag from the barman. It was ice-cold from being in the fridge all night. They left by the side door of the Clarendon bar, bracing themselves against the rain with their coats. Within minutes, they were walking towards the car park by the river. Claudia spotted Brendan's car from the glow of the taillights and a thin ribbon of smoke streaming out through the top of the driver's window. She furrowed her brow and then relaxed. Tonight she would say nothing.

Brendan recognised her walk instantly. In silhouette, her stride was unmistakable, like her mother's. Someone was with her, a lanky bugger at that, he thought. He took a deep breath and exhaled, trying to release his mood. Then he flicked the remains of his cigarette out into the rain. As they approached the bonnet, he put on a strained smile and reached over to pull the handle, opening the passenger door. Claudia climbed in. And as the guy slipped in behind them, Brendan noticed his head rubbing the roof. He heard the rustle of a plastic bag and smiled wryly to himself. What is it about kids nowadays? he thought. Can they not enjoy a pint or two without bringing home a carryout?

Once they were both seated, Claudia made the introductions. 'Stefan, this is Brendan, my dad. Brendan, this is Stefan.' Both men reached between the seats and shook hands awkwardly.

'Hallo.' Stefan's voice was deep.

'What's happening?' Brendan shrugged.

'Stefan has something for you.' Claudia raised her eyebrows.

Reaching forward through the seats, Stefan offered Brendan the plastic bag. Taking hold of the bag, Brendan had to lower it slightly, his grip surprised by the weight of the contents.

'*Alles Gute zum Geburtstag*!' Stefan announced.

Brendan was suddenly wrong-footed and without reply placed the bag on his lap. His thighs felt the shock as the slap of cold seeped through his jeans to his skin. He relaxed his grip, un-gathered the wrinkled plastic and peered inside. He couldn't see anything at first so he switched on the car courtesy light and widened the mouth of the bag, his eyes scanning the contents more carefully. A silver muscular body came slowly into view, glistening and wet. It was a fish; more than that, it appeared to be a wild salmon. He could smell the sea as his fingers traced the length of its form and he imagined the distances it must have travelled. He pictured a liquid landscape, a mass of shimmering light and envisioned shoals of salmon racing homeward.

'*Vielen Dank*, Stefan!' Brendan shook his head, a half-laugh disguising his embarrassed surprise. 'I don't understand. How did you get this?'

'This year, the river is teeming with them. We spent most of the day out by the Faughan,' Stefan said.

'So you're a bit of a fisherman?'

'Oh, yes! I came to Derry to study, to sing and to catch fish.' Stefan reached over and squeezed Claudia's arm.

'*Vielen Dank*! Really, thank you.' Brendan turned towards his daughter, leaned forward and kissed her cheek. Then, glancing at both of them, he spread out his arms, embracing Claudia with his right and hooking Stefan's shoulder through the gap in the seats with his left.

'Thank you both. I'm touched,' he said, smiling. 'So we're having salmon for my birthday. I think the occasion calls for a bit of music; what do you want to hear?'

'Funny you should say that,' Stefan said, taking a CD from his coat pocket. 'Do you want to hear something cool?'

YELLOW OCHRE

A fire burned in the grate, dissipating heat like a warm oven. As Conal's thumb moved, it traced a small arc on the arm of the chair. Polished by years of gentle friction, an amber streak blazed beneath the skin of varnish.

Today, like most days, Conal spent his time remembering distant moments of his life, like some deep-sea fish dreaming of the sky. Always, it seemed, when he replayed his past, the images were brighter, more vibrant than his life now. Somehow they were like a postcard world, the ones he had picked up here and there over the years, postcards by some photographer he had forgotten the name of who had taken shots of every county in Ireland. He recalled how they were hand tinted with beautiful blues, greens and yellows. And often Conal found himself longing for somewhere where the land was truly bright and the sky remained a sweeping blue. Strange, though, of all the colours, yellow was the one, the one that best expressed the vibrancy of his youth.

This afternoon, Conal was thinking of a particular day at Hollybush, his first school. The school was more like a little church, full of huddled souls under a high, timbered ceiling. The ceiling had darkened to a rich walnut hue with the lazy smoke from the open fire. He remembered his father's turf fuelled the flames that day. Outside, it was wet, blustery. Grey mist bled from the sky into the lough. The hedges were winter thin. The children gathered near the fire for heat. He remembered Miss Quigley opening a book of paintings to show the class. They all moved closer to the teacher, hoping to get a better view of the pictures in the book. The images used paint in mysterious ways. Some were created from different-coloured dots; others used collage and one was sculpted in bold, thick

135

strokes. The book was large and square and he stared in wonder as Miss Quigley lifted the book high for them all to see.

'Now, children, this was Vincent's last painting,' she said.

The painting was wide, like the landscape, the sky dark, a blue-black scattered with departing crows. It could have been Inishowen, Conal thought. The yellow paint was so thick and textured that he put his hand forward, his fingers anticipating a scale-like skin of paint. But the paper was smooth.

And for the first time, as if it knew him, Yellow spoke to him.

After that morning in school, everything began to sing its yellowness to him. He spent days, weeks and months rediscovering his own yellow fields. He noticed wild flowers, lesser celandine and creeping buttercups – even the flowering gorse bushes that quilted the small valleys around him. He welcomed the vibrancy of fresh thatch and the delight of a yellowhammer in an April hedge. The simple pleasure of butter waited like a dollop of pigment on his mother's table. Sometimes he imagined a world full of yellow spread out in bold thick smears. He could never decide if he wanted to live in it or eat it.

Conal raised himself slowly, his hands clamping each arm of the wooden chair. He swung himself up and out from the seat, using his shoulders as a pivot. At last standing, he composed himself and shuffled towards the fireplace. He stooped painfully, first to select and then to place some broken sods on the glowing hearth. As he did so, the smell from the burning turf wafted up and around his chest. He breathed, inhaling its musk.

Like the smoke, Conal's thoughts began to drift, drifting back to an evening in the 1930s. He was sitting with his grandfather at a small table under a low ceiling in a cottage in Greencastle. It was mid-July, about half past ten in the evening. They were having supper, tea with bread and homemade jam. He must have had four slices or more. Through the window, they watched the sun sink beneath the brown-black ridge of the turf stack. His grandfather drew his attention to the tablecloth as it turned from a pale peach to red and then red-blue. Then his grandfather began talking about paint.

'My little Bible,' he said, showing the gaps in his teeth as he laughed. From the pocket of his jacket hanging from the chair he withdrew a small book, opening it slowly like it was a wallet full of money.

'*Oil Painting for Beginners* by SJ Cartlidge,' he read, his finger tracing the embossed type on the cover. Then he thumbed to chapter two. 'Pigments,' he whispered as his finger rested under the black type. 'Cadmium yellow, raw sienna, yellow ochre,' he said as though it were a poem. 'Made from natural earth … it dries well, has a great body. When dry, it appears slightly darker than when freshly laid upon canvas.'

And young Conal relished that evening; the dying light, the hot tea and his grandfather's words until it seemed the memory had taken on the quality of paint.

Conal turned from the fire and moved in the poor light to where he knew the dresser stood. When he reached it, his fingers mapped the wood, creating its shape and familiar geometry in his head. He felt for the cool metal of the drawer handle, his thumb tracing the curved metal as his fingers gripped the brass. He tugged the drawer open. A soft bouquet of trapped scent – oil paint – was released into the air, drifting up towards his nose. The floor of the drawer held layers of unframed paintings, murky with charcoal and age. In the left corner sat a single turtle-shell button still trailing a black thread. Beside the button was a harmonica. To the right sat a bundle of old letters topped with a black-and-white photograph of a young couple. It was taken perhaps fifty or sixty years before.

They smiled out at him, but although he knew they were there, he could not see them.

His right hand pawed around in the space, like a cat just short of a mouse. Then he caught it and with a little effort coaxed and drew it out from the drawer. It was an old cigar box, a remnant of a gold crest and the words 'Padilla – 25

Lanceros 1932′ were barely visible on the lid. He held the box carefully in his hand while he levered open the tiny clasp. He listened for the sense of something sliding, shifting its weight to the edge. Bedded down in a cushion of cotton wool was the simple beauty of a magnifying glass. Touching the handle, it reminded him of his father's old razor and that clear day when he lifted the blade, wet and cold from the stained enamel sink. He saw himself again, soaping up with the stiff-haired wobbling brush, then scraping the soap from his cheeks and rinsing the metal under the gurgling tap. He had towelled his face and neck and stared back into the silver glass and dreamed of a chin like sandpaper.

Conal's finger and thumb circled the brass handle of the glass, searching for its centre of gravity. Lifting it free, he thought of its sharp eye. Today he wanted to see, to see the bird he kept in the cage near the window. Now and again he could hear its gentle mutterings. It seemed to tut as though weighing up the rights and wrongs of life as Conal's mother had done. It was as if it had decided some poor soul was getting a raw deal. But today Conal wanted more than the faint hint he could decipher from the hearth or the soft whisper of light he sensed from the window.

Edging towards the table, his eyes registered the growing brightness. He could hear the faintest of sounds as the bird shifted its weight. Stooping a little, he gradually lowered himself down into the stiff-backed chair and rested his elbows on the tablecloth. He raised the glass up to his eye. The white parallel lines of a small cage came into focus. Like filter paper, they seemed to sift him to the day when his grandniece came visiting. Even with his failing sight, his eyes caught something bright fluttering beneath her outstretched arm. He had been sitting out near the old daffodil beds. He remembered squinting intensely, eager to discover what it was. Brigitte had guided his hands into the cage until he held the bird in his palm. Against his trembling fingers it felt delicate as a moth. His heart lifted that day over a year ago as they both created a new home for his canary.

Suddenly, the bird appeared in the window of the lens, exuberant as an exotic flower. In that moment, the full force of the entire world's yellowness seemed to burst before him. He felt a charge of shock run through him. He was electrified, alive now, fully here, fully Conal. The detail was all there, the surge of colour, fluffed up, a yellow host. Conal marvelled at his canary. He imagined paint, a clot of yellow.

* * *

It was early evening when they found Conal lying beneath the table. The cage had snagged on his sleeve as he fell. Everything came down with him. The plastic casing clipped to the bottom of the cage had smashed, leaving the bird free to escape. Birdseed was scattered all around Conal's head like confetti. Ms Scullion had called earlier to collect the census form and thought she could see Conal's foot sticking out from under the chair. Neither she nor the sergeant who forced open the door noticed intermittent fluttering above the lintel.

A girl on a passing bus was tracing the word Brigitte in the condensation of the window. She waved vigorously in the direction of the open door as light from the hallway spilled out onto the lane. The escaping bird went unnoticed, its silhouette a tiny smudge in the blue-black of the evening sky. When the girl looked above the roof of the cottage, all she saw was a flock of departing crows.

* * *

A beam of light penetrated the dark heart of the room. It illuminated the right corner of a 1970s record player, a section of bleached floorboards and a lower left leg. The toes at the end of the leg were scrunching every few seconds. They drove the rocking motion of a bamboo chair. The leg was puffy, traversed by a network of varicose veins rising from the toes, over the arch of the foot, circling the ankle and climbing the calf. The flesh was bare all the way until it reached a pair of khaki shorts. The upper area of the shorts was partly covered by an olive-green singlet. The hot silence was interrupted by the sporadic sound of a single mosquito drifting in and out of the deep shadow of the room.

Lily was not young. She was not even middle-aged. But she was independent. She had grown tough, tougher than her skin had become after almost sixty years under a southern sun. She placed an empty beer bottle into the shadow to the right of her chair. A metallic-amber beetle crawled up the wet glass towards the label. After falling on its back a few times, it eventually moved on. Lily squashed it seconds later as her chair rocked forward. There was the faintest crunch, but she could not hear it.

She held an envelope flat against her belly. Her thumbs strummed the dog-eared flaps of paper where she had torn it open. So much of her life unfolded through these letters from Ireland. She held them as though they were the relics of some long-dead saint. The post-marked date and time set her picturing the scene the day the letters were posted. The little post office she encountered in her mind was one of the many ghosts from the world she'd left behind. It was surely gone now, but not in Lily's head. She pictured the dark wood counter of the tiny shop in Muff. The smells of old people as they entered, damp from the rain. She heard the sound of rain falling heavy, hitting the ground like stair rods as her father used to say. She missed the rain. She remembered the soft voices of Derry and East Donegal, their gossip, how they talked of brothers or cousins living in far-off lands.

'After all these years,' she said.

Her life was here now. New South Wales, Australia, was her home. As her fingers traced the torn paper edges, her thoughts strayed to the day when she had said goodbye to her father. They'd stood outside the Derry train station. Unconsciously, she had folded and unfolded her tickets. She was going to nurse her aunt in Wagga Wagga. Her father was awkward, not one for touching or hugging. He never displayed affection, even at the death of her mother ten years before. Everything was matter-of-fact with him.

'You have everything you need?' he said without a trace of emotion. It was a question, although it could have been a statement. It was as if she were just off to the village.

'Yes, Daddy,' Lily replied, knowing this was perhaps the last time they would meet or speak. For a moment, they held each other's uneasy gaze, the mutual silence dense as chapters. But as the rain soaked into the space between them, her father's shape seemed to drift away, dissolving into the structure of the Craigavon Bridge behind. She couldn't remember if they had said goodbye. Perhaps they had just spoken it in their heads. Then she had turned towards the platform and the train.

Lily stood up. It was a typical summer's day, over 40°C. No breeze, just relentless heat. She walked to the fridge and opened it. The interior illuminated her waist and breasts. They sagged now, her nipples pointing at her toes.

'Bugger, only three.' She sighed, counting the bottles in the fridge door. She lifted a Tooheys Old and with a quick twist of the bottle top, followed by a short hiss, she flicked the metal cap into a bucket on the floor.

'Bingo.' She raised a toast to the air as the cap hit the target, then tilted the bottle to her lips and necked a couple of mouthfuls. As she swallowed, she remembered her first taste. They had spent the day together on the coastal path between Moville and Greencastle. As usual, he was painting a stretch of beach. The wind was in his hair. Conal was expending his energy into the canvas. The smell of the sea was filling her nostrils. As she finished that first beer, it just popped into her head: a crazy thought! But Lily never cared what people thought. When she called him, he was so engrossed in an expanse of ochre he made no response. She called him again. This time he turned towards her, the palette knife between his teeth. Standing there, with just the sea and the gulls all around him, it could have been a film set. She was lying fully naked, her hips pressing the fine-grained sand, her ochre hair spilling

141

over her neck and shoulders. She could tell he was thinking paint. After perhaps a minute or so, he smiled and shouted, 'Lily, I need more ochre!'

Lily lifted an LP from a stack resting against the wall. The front cover had some green hills circling a small lake, a thatched, whitewashed cottage surrounded by trees in the foreground. The lettering was centred over a grey-blue sky. The title in bold type read THE GREAT JOHN MCCORMACK. She placed her beer on the wood veneer of the speaker, the wet bottle adding another circle to the pattern of rings in the dust. Gently, she rested the needle on track one.

'*The Kerry Dance, With Orchestra*, thirty-first of March nineteen thirty-six,' she whispered, then swallowed another gulp. Lily could only faintly hear the crackling voice as it rose out from the speakers into her room. She placed her hand against the black mesh of the box, her palm sensing the vibrating tones. A mosquito landed on her wrist and drank until the irritation caused her to look down.

'Drink, you little bastid,' she said and took another mouthful of beer. Her thoughts began to swim. Soon she was floating again in the cool, clear waters of Lough Foyle.

She had posed perhaps for a dozen paintings before it all came to a sudden end. She became the talk of the townland. People looked down when she passed on her bike. They were frightened of her.

'Lily Moore, brazen hussy,' she heard them say. 'She has the cheek to pose naked for a man … a man who isn't even her husband … and to do it in broad daylight … she is a sinful woman.'

Reverend Cunningham was leaving when Lily reached the lane leading home. He walked slowly without stopping, without looking up.

'Lily,' was all he said, lifting his hat slightly. She pressed into the hawthorn hedge as he passed, holding her finger against a thorn until it bled. This was it. It was real. She knew now, things would never be the same again. Her eyes followed the

silly little minister. She watched him continue out onto the wet
road and along the silhouette of trees, to the shore's edge.

That evening, she told her father that Conal had never
touched her.

'Not even to move an arm or a leg?' Her father laughed in
disbelief.

'Paint is his passion,' she said.

'Really? And what might yours be?'

By now, three bottles had been placed by the curve of the rocking chair. Currawongs were singing in the trees outside. Lily
walked to the screen door and looked out through the punc-
tured netting. The paddocks were bone dry, yellow-ochre as
straw. The bleached fence posts stretched the barbed wire like
musical strings. The two ghost gums she had planted decades
before stood silently, as if waiting for her.

Then it came to her. It just popped into her head. She
walked back to the record player, lifted the needle and placed
it on the last track. It was her mother's favourite, *Beautiful Isle
Of Somewhere*, from 1914. She turned the volume up to maximum and walked out onto the veranda, raising her singlet
past her ribs and breasts and up over her head. She dropped
her shorts and underwear, leaving them where they fell. Lily
stepped naked out onto the dry grass; she walked down past
the dunny, avoiding the bull ants, until she was knee-deep in
the dry, ochre landscape.

Hazy, shallow hills rolled southwards alongside the Murrumbidgee River. The sky was big, not like Ireland, but wide,
expansive, like the land itself. The sound of the lyrics drifted unevenly over the paddocks: *land of the true, where we live
anew*. They roamed far off towards the horizon, unhindered
until they were only traces of themselves. Lily sat down in the
grass, placed the letter on her lap, unfolded it and began to
read it again, this time aloud:

'Dear Lily, we are so very sorry to break the sad news to
you. Conal died peacefully in his home on the first day of

November nineteen ninety-eight. Among his belongings we found some letters and paintings. These should be with you soon. However, among his things we found this photograph of you both. It was taken shortly before you left. We thought you would like to have it.'

The photograph was of them standing together beside one of the old changing shelters along the shoreline path a little beyond Moville. They were clearly happy. On the reverse side, written in faded fountain pen, were the words 'Conal – Lily, Yellow – Ochre, July 1946'.

She set the photograph and the letter down on the ground and eased herself gently backwards until she was lying full-length in the grass. She placed her hands behind her head and presented her naked body to the afternoon sun. Smiling broadly, she said, 'Conal, you'll need more Flake White this time. Now, when you're ready, just paint me!'

Dreaming of the Sea

In the town of Stary Sącz, where Maja lived with her father, she had noticed that people looked at her strangely. One day, she threw a twig into the Poprad and watched it catch the current and flow downstream. She caught a glimpse of her own reflection and was struck by how thin she looked. Her skin was so pale that she thought perhaps she might be invisible. Then Maja developed a habit of blessing herself. And in the evening she liked to watch the sun travel behind the bell-tower on the roof of the convent. When its fire had disappeared below the Beskid Sądecki Mountains, sometimes she would imagine that God was calling her name. And Maja would tilt her head to the right and listen intently. It was 1999. It was also the year her mother died of leukaemia. Maja was ten years old.

* * *

When she was twelve, her father took her on a train journey to the Salt Mine in Wieliczka, near Kraków.

'You know, in the thirteenth century, Blessed Kinga brought a team of Hungarian miners to this very spot. They dug deep shafts into the earth until one day they saw something glisten in the darkness. It was something precious, hidden,' her father told her.

'What was it, Tata? What did they find?' Maja asked.

'They found Kinga's wedding ring buried in the rocks.'

And Maja smiled. Then they walked down all four hundred steps of the wooden stairway to the Chapel of Blessed Kinga, one hundred and fifty metres below. Maja threw her head backwards to look up at the rock-salt chandeliers. They sparkled like diamonds above her. She stared at them until she felt her balance shift and her father had to place his hand on her back to steady her.

'What are you thinking, Maja?'

'Do you think that somewhere there might be a jewel waiting for me?' Her eyes were fixed on the chandeliers.

'Oh, indeed there is, Maja.'

'Really?'

'Of course. And I know where it is.'

'Where? Where is it, Tata?'

'Ah, now that would be telling.'

'Please,' she said.

'You really don't know?' Her father smiled, prolonging the play.

'Tata, tell the truth. You're just teasing me.' Maja frowned.

'But everyone has one, including you.'

'Then tell me, Tata. Please, where is it?'

'Only if you close your eyes first.'

And Maja did as her father told her.

'Now, Maja, I want you to stand on your tiptoes and stretch your arms up as high as you can.'

With her eyes tightly closed, she lifted her heels free of the ground and raised her arms up above her head towards the chandeliers.

'I want you to imagine you are reaching back up through the shafts, out past the entrance to the mine, higher even than the branches of the trees outside until you are almost touching the blue of the sky.'

Maja pulled her belly tight against her spine, lifting her ribs upwards. Her arms strained for maximum reach until her fingertips quivered in the air above her.

'Please, Tata, tell me. Where is it?'

Suddenly, her father tickled her belly vigorously, catching her in his arms as she buckled in surprise.

'It's in there,' he said.

And Maja laughed so loud it echoed all around them, out beyond the steps and up through the shaft.

* * *

At seventeen, Maja began to rise early in the morning and stare wistfully out of her window towards the convent. One day after school, she took the route past the oak tree at the edge of the churchyard. She gazed up at the face of Saint Kinga's statue in the branches. After running towards the tall wooden doors, she slipped into the silence of the monastery where she marvelled at the vaulted ceiling, the icons and the white marble angels. And around the sculpted centrepiece of Saint Kinga, the radiating gold rays captivated her. That evening, the whisper of Maja's prayers mingled with the sound of simmering mushrooms as they stewed with tomatoes, boiled cabbage and smoked meat. Her father opened the kitchen door, letting the flavours of the *bigos* drift through the house until they reached her. And the rich aroma from the stove drew her out of her bedroom and down to her supper.

'Tata, do you remember the salt mine in Wieliczka?' she said as they ate.

'Still reaching for that jewel?' her father joked.

'I've been thinking.' Maja fiddled with a silver cross at her neck.

Her father took a mouthful of food, set his fork gently on the table and reached for the fingers of her left hand.

'This will always be your home, Maja. You know that,' he said. Maja leaned over and embraced him to the sound of the wall-clock ticking above them.

Barely a year later, the day came when she walked out into the autumn sunshine. Her father climbed the stairs to Maja's room and from the window watched her disappear beneath the tower gate of the Poor Clare Convent.

* * *

In the grip of winter, Sister Franciszka, as Maja became known, woke from a disturbed sleep. A full moon illuminated a small wooden crucifix on the wall beside her bed. It cast a long, oblique shadow that reached down to her pillow. Sister Franciszka stared out at the moon, and through a crack in a window she heard a dog bark in the empty streets below. As she listened she imagined it echoing out beyond the surrounding villages and up towards the foothills of the mountains. She remembered the times her father had taken her hiking in the Tatra Mountains. He had told Maja that lynx and wolves still roamed the forests. He'd shown her the telltale signs of brown bear. And Sister Franciszka began to feel trapped. As the weeks grew into months and opened into seasons, she yearned to experience the world beyond the convent, the Beskid Sądecki Mountains and Poland. But she told no-one, not even her God.

'You're barely flesh, Sister. Are you eating enough?' Mother Helena asked one day as she returned from the orchard. Sister Franciszka was tending the vegetable plot and her bent figure appeared bony as the wind caught her habit. She could have been a scarecrow. But Sister Franciszka casually pulled a fist of beetroot from the wet earth, their fine tendrils trailing in the mud.

'Only the freshest, Mother,' Maja replied.

'You look pale. Are you well?' Mother Helena asked.

'Yes, Mother,' Maja said and returned to her work. In truth, she felt ill; she had a dull ache low in her belly, but she ignored it. When her basket was full, she returned to the kitchen and began preparing the beetroot for the evening soup. In recent weeks, she was finding it difficult to eat without later having pain. And if she drank anything – even a glass of water – there were times when nothing stayed down. But she learned to hide her episodes of sickness. And so, just before her twentieth birthday, she fell gravely ill. Mother Helena was sent for. And when she entered Sister Franciszka's room and saw how the bed-sheet held the frailness of her frame, she sent for Doctor Janowski.

'The trees all along the valley are turning gold,' Doctor Janowski said when he arrived.

'The Lord brings beauty with every season. Come in, Doctor, you're most welcome.' Mother Helena opened the creaking door wide.

'The snows will soon be with us. Perhaps it will be minus twenty, like last year.' Doctor Janowski set his bag on the small table and removed his hat, scarf and overcoat.

'If the river freezes, the whole town will be skating along the Poprad,' Mother Helena commented, hanging his things on the stand by the door.

'Tell me, Mother, did the orchard deliver well this year?'

'Another bounty. You'll have a slice of szarlotka with your herbata?' she asked the doctor.

'I don't want to steal the food from your mouths.' He rubbed his hands briskly.

'I'm sure we can spare some tea and cake.'

'If you insist, Mother. Thank you, that would be nice. Now, where is our suffering saint?'

'It's Sister Franciszka, one of our young noviciates.'

Doctor Janowski followed Mother Helena up the narrow oak stairs leading to the bedrooms. He whistled tunelessly in anticipation of his apple cake.

Later, when the examination was over, the doctor looked directly into Sister Franciszka's expectant face. She sensed concern in his eyes as he placed his hand under his chin and played with the hairs of his goatee.

'What's wrong with me, Doctor?'

'Well, there are a number of possibilities. But to be truthful, I'm not sure.'

'Is it serious?'

The doctor unhooked the stethoscope from his neck, folded the rubber tube against the metal arms and began to slowly return his instruments to his bag. After he closed the bag, he paused. Sister Franciszka sensed he was choosing his words carefully.

'You know ... the mind and the body, they are so intricately connected.' He paused. Then after a moment, 'Is something troubling you, Sister?' Gently, he placed his right hand on Sister Franciszka's forearm.

Sister Franciszka avoided his eyes and gazed out the window at the heavy autumn sky. She gave no reply.

'I'd like you to think about it. Could you do that for me?' he said.

Sister Franciszka turned to face him. 'Yes.'

'Good,' he said, instantly brighter and patting her forearm with his palm. 'I'll write you a referral for the hospital in Kraków. After they've carried out a few tests, we'll have a clearer picture then.'

'Should I arrange another appointment?'

'In a fortnight or so. But try not to worry. I'm sure everything's fine. Now, please forgive me, Sister. I have a pressing engagement with a slice of Mother Helena's szarlotka.' Doctor Janowski chuckled as he rose from his chair.

By the time she arrived at Kraków, Sister Franciszka had developed a fever. She was admitted, told to undress and asked to slip on a hospital gown. She was placed on a bed. Moments later, she was wheeled through a network of corridors clogged with people on trolleys. Eventually, she reached the X-ray department. But she had to wait. There was a long queue. After a while, she fell asleep.

There was a sudden jolt as a trolley-bed bumped the side of her mattress and she woke. A flurry of nurses appeared. It was followed by the sound of a man groaning fitfully in pain. He was hidden beneath a jumble of bloodstained sheets. Every few seconds, his arms flailed loosely about him as though wrestling, fending off an attack. It took three nurses to restrain him before the doctor arrived and the injection he administered took effect. The man's bed was so close to Sister Franciszka's that she could smell the sweat of his body. It was musky and vivid. Unconsciously, she was drawn to him. Caked in blood and covered with gravel dust, his right arm suddenly burst from the confines of his bed and made a grab at her gown.

'I'm alive. I'm fucking alive!' he roared, his gaze fixed on her blanched face. Her hand clasped around his wrist and she felt his pulse throb rapidly against her thumb. And in that moment, what Sister Franciszka saw reflected in the sapphire of his eyes was that the path of her life was a mistake. She had given away everything, even her name. The man relaxed his grip and attempted to thrust his fist into the air. But seconds later, his arm dangled limp between the beds. Abruptly, an orderly appeared and pushed the man's bed down the corridor, wheeling him briskly into the X-ray room. Sister Franciszka noticed overalls trailing precariously from a corner of the bed frame as it disappeared behind the flapping doors.

'What happened to him?' she asked as one of the nurses hurried past.

'Mining accident. One of the lucky ones,' the nurse replied.

Sister Franciszka flopped back down onto her pillow and sighed heavily, her legs manoeuvring under the bedclothes for comfort. The sheet was folded tightly under the base of the mattress and she felt suddenly confined. Something heavy registered against her left foot, a medical file or clipboard perhaps. When she glanced down to check, it was a book. Intrigued, she reached down and picked it up. The book was well thumbed, covered in a film of fine dust and grit and curled in on itself as though it had been rolled into a tight pocket. She read the title, *Lonely Planet, IRELAND*. Turning to the first page, she saw a name written in biro on the top right-hand corner, *Lucjan Kaminski*. Below the name was a mobile telephone number, but the dirt and grime obscured the last three digits.

* * *

'I'm proud of you, Maja,' her father told her.

'Tata, please! Don't keep saying that. I'm really not sure what I feel.' Maja shook her head.

'It can't have been easy. Your mother, she would have understood,' her father continued.

'Mama's dead, Tata!' She slapped the table hard with her hand.

Her father dropped his gaze and began to fiddle with the crumbs scattered over the surface of the breadboard. He drew them into a loose pile.

'I'm sorry, Tata.' She reached out to touch his hand.

'It's fine. You're bound to be upset after reaching such a big decision.'

'I'm so confused, I feel completely lost.'

Her father cupped both his hands over her fingers. 'You're freezing. You feeling okay?'

'I'm fine.'

'What exactly did Janowski say about the tests?'

'Just that they'd found some inflammation but it was nothing to worry about, nothing serious.'

'That's good news, don't you think?' Her father's face brightened.

'Yes. But now I have an emotional problem, or so he thinks,' she said, lifting her eyebrows.

'You've spoken to Mother Helena. It must be a relief. You'll be on the mend now. You'll see.'

'I feel like I've let everyone down.'

'Maja, you made a mistake. So what? Don't we all?'

'I made a fool of myself,' Maja said.

'Honestly, you mustn't think that! If anything, it's the opposite. You had the courage to change course. That takes real character.'

'You think so?' she said, looking into his eyes.

'I know so, Maja. You followed your heart. You tried the religious life. It wasn't for you. You did the right thing. You left. Next chapter. Anyway, I'm glad.'

'Why?' Maja looked at her father in disbelief.

'Before your mother died, I promised I'd respect her wishes. It's no secret: religion was never my thing. Anyway, Poland is part of a wider world now. And, Maja, you've so much to offer,' he said. Then he gently rocked her hands in his. They looked at each other in silence.

'For a long time I felt so trapped. I thought I would never be able to leave,' she said, holding back tears. 'I just couldn't find the strength to tell anyone.'

'Your body spoke for you.'

She nodded, her eyes brimming. For a few moments they didn't speak.

'But you've forgotten something,' her father said.

'What?'

He cocked both his forefingers and pointed towards her belly. Then he nodded.

'In there,' he said.

'My jewel.' Maja gave a reluctant smile.

'The one and only.'

Maja leaned back in her chair, drew her arms up from the table and ran her fingers through her cropped black hair.

'Now what? What do I do now?' she said.

'Go with the flow.'

'Of what, exactly?'

'Your life.'

'What does that mean, Tata? I've wasted so much time already. I'll have to start over. Doing what, living where?'

'Maja, you're only in your twenties. I know it's an old cliché, but go out there and find yourself. Travel!' Her father gestured to the world beyond the view of the window.

Maja leaned forward, placed her elbows on the table and propped up her chin with the palm of her right hand.

'Do you remember when I was little I used to drop twigs in the Poprad to see if they would float? I just loved watching them catch the current.'

'Dreaming of the sea,' he said. 'Even then.'

'You know, I like that.'

'Well?'

'Well what?'

'Set sail.'

'Tata, it's not that simple.'

'Why not? You've nothing to lose. Besides, I've seen that book in your room.'

155

'You mean Ireland? The *Lonely Planet* thing?'

'Okay, it's a Bible of sorts, I'll give you that. But it's certainly not a novel.' He laughed. 'And anyway, who's Lucjan Kaminski?' he said, teasing her.

'You've been snooping in my room, Tata. Honestly, even Mother Helena wouldn't have done such a thing.' Maja assumed a pose of mock protest.

'I couldn't help it. I was replacing the light bulb. The book was on your bedside table, all curled up. I saw the name.'

'Good excuse,' she said. 'Well, if you must know, someone accidentally dropped it on my bed when I was at the hospital last month.'

'Some people might say there are no accidents.'

'Believe me, Tata, this was an accident.'

'In that case, it's theft,' he teased.

'Not quite, I'm just borrowing it for a while. Well, until I've read it at least.'

'If it's a guidebook, why not use it as one? Ireland is certainly surrounded by the sea. The untamed Atlantic,' he said.

'You're crazy.'

'Put it this way, if the book is on loan, then it has to be returned,' he said. 'After you come back, you can always look this Lucjan up and tell him what Ireland is really like.'

'Tata, I'm trying to find myself, not a man, remember?'

'True. But it would be good for you to travel, experience somewhere new. Head off for a couple of months. Don't you think?'

'Well, it's tempting.'

'If you go in the spring, it would give me time to help with the cost.'

'Are you serious?' she said.

Later, Maja and her father stood looking over the side of the Wegeirska Bridge that straddled the road heading north to Nowy Sącz. It was a cool, clear November day. There was a light breeze. Maja had four wine-bottle corks in a brown paper bag. Each had a cocktail stick embedded in its top supporting a tiny paper flag. They looked like toy yachts, like a child might make in play to race down the river. There was a flag for each of the four compass points of Ireland: Derry, the north, was red; Cork, the south, was green; Dublin, the east, was yellow; and Galway, the west, was blue.

'Whichever flag appears first on the other side ...' her father said.

'You're really going to pay for the ticket?' she asked.

'I should have enough by spring.'

'Are we ready, then?'

'And long may she sail,' her father joked.

When Maja looked down onto the surface of the river, she caught a glimpse of her own reflection and was struck by how happy she looked. Tipping the contents of the bag over the edge, she watched as they tumbled and flipped in the cold, clear air until they plopped into the waters of the Poprad. They bobbed briefly, then bumped and swirled around the smooth, wet stones. Soon they began to drift, then flow swiftly beneath the shadows of the bridge. Maja swung round, grabbed hold of her father's hand and raced across the road. As they reached the opposite footpath, she let go of his fingers and rushed forward, clamping her elbows over the metal railing of the bridge. Eagerly, she gazed down onto the flowing waters of the river.

'Come on!' she cried.

'Can you see anything?' her father shouted as he caught up.

'Not yet! Any second now.'

Then smoothly, the corks sailed into view.

'Hold on. Yes!' Maja clapped her hands in excitement.

'Which one's in the lead?'

'They're still in the shadow, Tata. Wait till the sunlight catches them ...'

'Looks to be neck-and-neck to me, Maja.'

Then one of them flared and glistened as it slipped into the clear winter light.

'It's red! It's definitely red! I've forgotten, Tata. Which city did we say was red?'

Her father drew a piece of paper from his coat pocket and quickly checked the list of names against the flag colours.

'Derry. The red one is Derry,' he declared.

'Is that the Walled City?' Maja asked.

'The City of Culture, it says here.'

'Well, Derry it is,' Maja said, raising her arms in the winter sun.